W9-AXX-903

"Signor dei Cesari, please be reasonable."

Beth stopped struggling and deliberately dropped her voice. "Why wouldn't I tell you if I knew? But I don't. All I know is that Giles is somewhere in Europe on business." Her blue eyes implored him. "Believe me, that's the truth."

"The truth, signorina? Are you perfectly certain?"

"I wouldn't lie to you," she told him.

"Oh, no, signorina?" He raised one black eyebrow. "I do not believe you. After all, you are a woman. Lies and women go together like pasta and Parmesan. Unfortunately deceit is part of the female's nature, especially when you are dealing with men." He paused for a moment and let his eyes roam over her. "Signorina, you are lying now."

Stephanie Howard is a British author whose two ambitions since childhood were to see the world and to write. Her first venture into the world was a four-year stay in Italy, learning the language and supporting herself by writing short stories. Then her sensible side brought her back to London to study Social Administrations at the London School of Economics. She has held various editorial posts at magazines such as *Reader's Digest*, *Vanity Fair* and *Women's Own*. She has also written free-lance for *Cosmopolitan*, *Good Housekeeping* and the *Observer*.

Books by Stephanie Howard

HARLEQUIN ROMANCE

3093—MASTER OF GLEN CRANNACH
3112—AN IMPOSSIBLE PASSION
3153—WICKED DECEIVER
3195—ROMANTIC JOURNEY

HARLEQUIN PRESENTS

1098—RELUCTANT PRISONER
1130—DARK LUCIFER
1168—HIGHLAND TURMOIL
1273—BRIDE FOR A PRICE
1307—KISS OF THE FALCON
1450—A BRIDE FOR STRATHALLANE

Don't miss any of our special offers. Write to us at the following address for information on our newest releases.

Harlequin Reader Service
P.O. Box 1397, Buffalo, NY 14240
Canadian address: P.O. Box 603,
Fort Erie, Ont. L2A 5X3

A MATTER OF HONOUR
Stephanie Howard

Harlequin Books

TORONTO • NEW YORK • LONDON
AMSTERDAM • PARIS • SYDNEY • HAMBURG
STOCKHOLM • ATHENS • TOKYO • MILAN
MADRID • WARSAW • BUDAPEST • AUCKLAND

If you purchased this book without a cover you should be aware that this book is stolen property. It was reported as "unsold and destroyed" to the publisher, and neither the author nor the publisher has received any payment for this "stripped book."

Original hardcover edition published in 1991
by Mills & Boon Limited

ISBN 0-373-03220-X

Harlequin Romance first edition September 1992

A MATTER OF HONOUR

Copyright © 1991 by Stephanie Howard.
All rights reserved. Except for use in any review, the reproduction or utilization of this work in whole or in part in any form by any electronic, mechanical or other means, now known or hereafter invented, including xerography, photocopying and recording, or in any information storage or retrieval system, is forbidden without the permission of the publisher, Harlequin Enterprises Limited, 225 Duncan Mill Road, Don Mills, Ontario, Canada M3B 3K9.

All the characters in this book have no existence outside the imagination of the author and have no relation whatsoever to anyone bearing the same name or names. They are not even distantly inspired by any individual known or unknown to the author, and all incidents are pure invention.

® are Trademarks registered in the United States Patent and Trademark Office and in other countries.

Printed in U.S.A.

CHAPTER ONE

BETH sensed who the man was the instant she caught sight of him standing tall and broad-shouldered beside the big bright red sun-umbrella. And, though his face was in shadow, she knew he was watching her.

She cursed beneath her breath as she stepped out of the shallows, a slim supple figure in an elegant black swimming-suit, and paused to squeeze the water from her shoulder-length blonde hair. Beth had never met him, but she had heard a great deal about him, and not a single word of it had been favourable. His arrival here on this deserted stretch of beach, she would lay money, was no accident.

Yet what could he possibly want with her?

Beth had left her sandals at the edge of the water before embarking on her swim. She slipped them on now, feeling the hot sand scorch her toes, and walked unhurriedly towards the big red sun-umbrella—*her* big red sun-umbrella, where she had left all her things!—resisting the urge to shade her eyes with her hand so that she could see the man more clearly. The bright southern-Italian sun was dazzling, but she had no wish to reveal that she was curious.

She stopped a metre or so away from him and demanded in a cool tone, 'Is there something I can do for you?'

He was dressed all in white—trousers, shirt and shoes—the sleeves of the shirt rolled back to his elbows to reveal strongly muscled, mahogany-dark forearms. And the way his hands were pushed arrogantly into his pockets, broad shoulders thrust back, long legs planted apart, lent him a faint but distinct air of menace.

It was him all right, Beth felt with growing certainty. The very man she had hoped to avoid during her mission-of-mercy visit to Muretto.

'Did you enjoy your swim?' He ignored her question. 'In this heat the sea is the best place to be.'

Beth narrowed her eyes at him. 'It was very pleasant.' Then, politely but firmly, she reminded him, 'I asked you if there was anything I could do for you?'

'Yes, I heard you, *signorina.*' With a flicker of a smile, he let his gaze travel over her creamy-skinned figure, voluptuously moulded by the dripping-wet swim-suit. 'And I'm sure, if I put my mind to it, I could think of something.' Then, with the lift of one eyebrow, his gaze returned to her face with its wide blue eyes and firm determined chin. 'Did you have anything particular in mind?'

'As a matter of fact, I didn't.' Beth's response was swift and cutting. It would take more than that sort of provocative needling to discomfit her, it advised him.

But he merely smiled. 'That's a pity. A waste of a splendid opportunity.'

Close to, he was even taller than he had appeared from a distance, with a head of carelessly brushed back hair as black and as glossy as polished jet. And, though she still could not make out his features clearly because of the sun that shone in her eyes, Beth was aware of a face of craggy hard lines—strong curved nose, firm jutting chin. And she was aware, too, of the message it spoke to the world.

Take me or leave me, his face announced without compromise. Either way, I don't give a damn!

Very much my own feelings right now, Beth thought grimly. If he had come here to make trouble he would soon discover that she was in no mood to be trampled on. She smiled to herself wryly. How she had changed! Over the past few weeks the usually mild-mannered Beth had become something of an expert at standing up for herself!

Still, she kept her tone mild as she continued to confront him. 'Are you going to tell me what you want of me? I take it you're waiting here for a purpose?' The last thing she needed right now was more problems. All she really wanted was for him to leave.

But he didn't move a muscle. 'Do I need a reason to be here? Perhaps I was simply admiring the view.'

As he said it his eyes flickered over her once more, and Beth felt a dart of irritation. Her tone sharpened as she advised him, 'Then I suggest you go and admire the view elsewhere. This stretch of beach happens to be private!'

'Is it, indeed?' A pair of shadowed eyes looked back at her. 'Then perhaps you ought to explain to me what you're doing here.'

'And why should I do that?'

'Because you are not one of the villa residents to whom this stretch of beach belongs. If you were, I can assure you, I would know you. I make it my business to acquaint myself with the residents.'

So I've heard, Beth observed to herself scathingly. From what she'd been told, he did more than just acquaint himself. He made a point of sticking his nose into everyone's business!

She looked into his face, squaring her slim shoulders. 'Well, you don't have to worry. I'm here quite legitimately. I happen to be a guest of one of the residents.'

'May I enquire which one?'

He was living up to his reputation! 'I don't really see what that has to do with you.'

She saw a flicker of annoyance cross his face. Clearly, he was unaccustomed to having his right to ask questions challenged. Then he smiled at her coldly. 'Your co-operation is unnecessary. I already know that you're a guest of Giles Portman.'

'So, if you knew, why did you ask?'

'Out of politeness.'

Beth smiled at him mockingly. Out of deviousness, more likely! But, before she could say anything, he observed in a scathing tone, 'You're one of his girlfriends, I expect?'

'No, I'm not one of his girlfriends,' Beth corrected him icily, resenting the undercurrent of contempt in the question. It had been intended as an insult both to Giles and to herself.

She glared across at him, disdaining to enlighten him as to her true relationship with Giles. It was none of his business that they were stepbrother and sister. Giles had been right. This man was odious!

'So, now that you know that I'm not an interloper, perhaps you wouldn't mind leaving,' she suggested tightly. 'I was really rather enjoying my privacy.'

'My apologies.' He smiled with evident insincerity and pointedly made no move to go. Instead, he informed her, 'Alas, now that I know you are the person I was seeking, I must deprive you of your privacy for a moment or two more.' He gestured to the sunbed in the shade of the sun-umbrella. 'Please. You may as well make yourself comfortable while we talk.'

'I'm quite comfortable where I am.' Beth glared at him defiantly. It went totally against the grain to do this man's bidding! Nor did she

wish to prolong their meeting. She had come here
to Muretto on some private family business, not
to become embroiled with this local big-shot who,
according to her stepbrother, positively enjoyed
making himself a thorn in innocent people's
sides!

She flashed angry blue eyes at him. 'What do
you want of me? Just tell me that. That's all I
want to know.'

He ignored her demand as though it had never
been spoken. 'Suit yourself, *signorina cara*.
Personally, I prefer the shade. The sun at this
hour is rather fierce.' He reached for the little
folding stool at the side of the sunbed where Beth
had laid out her sun-creams and things, which
he scooped up and laid on the sunbed without
so much as a by-your-leave. 'I also prefer sitting
when I'm having a conversation.' And with
arrogant disdain for her bristling disapproval he
lowered his tall frame on to the stool.

'And who said we were having a conversation?' Beth folded her arms across her chest.
'Just tell me what you've come for, then kindly
leave!'

'I shall leave in good time.' His eyes met hers
and she was aware of a flicker of dark hostility
that sent a sudden cold dart down her spine.
Then, unexpectedly, he smiled and once more
pointed to the sunbed. 'The sooner we talk the
sooner you'll be free of me.'

'Very well, then. Talk.' She ignored his invitation. 'I can hear you perfectly from here.'

He shook his head at her. 'You're being foolish. You'll burn if you insist on staying out there. Do as I say. Come and sit in the shade.' His eyes bored into her as he waited for her to obey.

He was right, of course. Even as she stood there in the full glare of the midday Mediterranean sun, Beth could feel her delicate English skin begin to tighten uncomfortably and burn. Yet her stubborn streak made her resist a moment longer, her eyes conveying the message that, in any other circumstances, all the bullying in the world would not have persuaded her to give in to him.

Then, without looking at him, she swept past him and sat down on the sunbed, snatched up her beach-towel and rubbed vigorously at her hair. 'Well?' she demanded briskly. 'Carry on. I'm waiting.'

He smiled across at her. 'Now we're both comfortable,' he observed.

That was not strictly true. Beth felt unaccountably uneasy. There was something about his closeness that both worried her and troubled her. And those feelings of unease were compounded by the fact that, now that the light was no longer in her eyes, she could see his features at last quite clearly.

Their dark rugged lines were even harsher in this light, the wide mobile mouth betraying a nature of fierce passions, the smooth, high brow a prodigious intelligence. But it was his eyes, which before had been in shadow, that now totally dominated his face. They were ferocious eyes, glittering and savage, as dark as midnight, as mysterious as the cosmos, and with the power to draw one's gaze like a magnet.

And the eyes, too, blazed out a message to the world. Tread cautiously, they warned, if tread you must!

Beth snatched her gaze away, the gesture self-protective. There was something a little unsettling about the power behind those eyes.

She could feel them on her. 'Before we proceed, I think I should introduce myself,' he was saying. Then, as Beth turned to glare at him, he extended one hand towards her. 'My name is dei Cesari. Lorenzo dei Cesari. You and I, *signorina*, are neighbours.'

So she had been absolutely right! He was who she had thought he was! Not that that knowledge gave her much solace.

She ignored his outstretched hand. 'There's no need for formalities. I already know who you are,' she informed him.

'No doubt you do.' There was iron in his voice. 'No doubt Giles has told you all about me.'

'He has mentioned you, yes.' She smiled sardonically, her eyes conveying that what she had heard was not good.

His own eyes were like splinters. 'I can well imagine. But, take my advice, don't believe all you're told—especially from so suspect and unreliable a source.'

'Oh, don't worry, I'm quite capable of making up my own mind,' Beth assured him, tossing aside her towel. 'But, so far, I have no reason to believe Giles's judgement to be unreliable. On the contrary——' she smiled sweetly '—it accords perfectly with my own.'

He didn't bat an eyelid, just looked back at her impassively and once more extended his hand towards her. 'But you have still not introduced yourself, *signorina*. You have not done me the honour of telling me your name.'

His unshakeable poise was deeply infuriating. Beth combed back her wet hair with her fingers and responded with barely concealed irritation, 'I'm surprised you find an introduction necessary. Since you came here deliberately to find me, I'm sure you already know who I am.'

Giles had told her that dei Cesari knew all the village business, that he kept people on his payroll to keep him informed. 'Don't tell me that your spies have failed to supply you with such basic information?' she taunted.

'Apparently they have—but they have had very little time. After all, you only arrived in Muretto last night.' There was amusement in his tone as he answered her now. The black eyes had softened, the mouth quirked with humour. 'All I was told was that a beautiful young woman had moved into Mr Portman's villa. Alas, they weren't able to supply your name.'

He could change like the wind, Beth thought with a small shiver, and his flattery was as

powerful and as lethal as his hostility. Had she
not known to his detriment the kind of man he
was, this sudden display of charm might have
disarmed her.

As it was, his dark eyes seemed to mesmerise
her as he now demanded silkily, 'So, will you tell
me? Will you grant me the favour of telling me
your name?'

Beth tore her gaze away. This man was
dangerous. 'My name is Beth Carson,' she answered in clipped tones. But, almost uncon-
sciously, she had reached out to clasp his hand,
feeling the blood leap within her as his flesh
pressed against her flesh. Hurriedly she withdrew
her strangely tingling fingers.

'In a small place like Muretto, news tends to
travel fast. And the arrival of a newcomer is
always a matter of great interest. Especially when
that newcomer is an unaccompanied young
female.'

As he spoke he faced her squarely from his
stool, hands propped lightly on his spread-apart
knees, his body slightly bent towards her, his
demeanour open, inviting her confidence. And
yet behind this amiable façade Beth could sense
the unyielding core of steel in him. If he was out
to win her over, there had to be a reason, and it
most assuredly was not because he wanted her to
like him. She had already judged that he didn't
give a damn, not for her opinion of him, nor for
anybody else's.

She watched him closely as he put to her, still in that warm seductive tone, 'So, what are you doing here, Miss Carson? I understood that Giles was away at the moment.'

So, he knew that too. 'Yes, he is. It's rather nice having the villa all to myself,' she declared evasively.

'But not for long, surely? Surely he would not leave you alone here? That would be rather inhospitable.'

'Please don't worry about it,' Beth assured him, sensing that behind his polite enquiry lay a deeper, far less casual curiosity. And there was no one in the world she was less likely to discuss Giles with—or the highly personal business with him that had brought her here.

She threw him a blank smile. 'I'm sure that Giles will do what's right.'

'I admire your faith.' His gibe was predictable. He appeared to hate Giles as much as Giles hated him. And it suddenly struck Beth, as she looked into his eyes, that she would not for all the world want to swap places with Giles. Lorenzo dei Cesari was an unwise choice for an enemy.

'He does know you're here?'

The question surprised her. Taken unawares, Beth felt herself flush. 'Of course he knows I'm here,' she lied quickly, looking back at him, suddenly feeling guilty beneath the power of that dark gaze.

Which was ridiculous, she rationalised. She had no reason to feel guilty. Although she had come here without Giles's knowledge, she and her family had a key to the villa and an open invitation to visit whenever they chose. And, besides, the current circumstances were very special.

'You're absolutely sure that you're telling me the truth?' With his sharp eyes he had picked up that guilty blush of hers.

'Absolutely sure,' she insisted without a flicker. To admit otherwise would involve her in all sorts of explanations, none of which concerned him in the slightest.

'Not that I care whether he knows you're here or not.' Lorenzo dei Cesari sat back on his stool, stretching his long legs out before him. 'For all I care you could be some spurned and jealous girlfriend come to cut the contents of his wardrobe into pieces.' He smiled across at her with sadistic humour. 'That is, I believe, a favourite pastime of spurned girlfriends.'

'I'm afraid I wouldn't know. It would appear that you're the expert.' She smiled, rather enjoying the image that that conjured up.

He smiled back at her enigmatically, then let his eyes drift seawards, presenting her with a glimpse of a hard dark profile. For a moment he seemed to study the shimmering horizon where a couple of small vessels danced and bobbed, then he turned his gaze back on her, bright as a searchlight. 'So, you have not come to bring an erring boyfriend to book?'

'I've already told you I'm not Giles's girlfriend.'

'No,' he corrected her, 'what you told me was that you were not *one* of his girlfriends. For all I know, you may believe yourself to be special. That would be foolish.' His eyes seemed to darken. 'Mr Giles Portman has many girlfriends, I assure you!'

'That's his business. He's a single man.' Beth looked into his face, wondering at his disapproval. Surely he was guilty of at least equal profligacy? For it was impossible to imagine a man like Lorenzo dei Cesari, with all that aggressive male vitality he exuded, leading a celibate or even sexually restrained life.

As the thought uncurled inside her, she almost blushed again. There was something rather tantalising about the thought of him as a lover.

She pulled herself up short. What in heaven's name had got into her? What kinds of thoughts were these to be having?

He was leaning towards her, dark eyes surveying her. 'So, if you are not his girlfriend, what is your relationship? Somehow I can't imagine that you're just a good friend.' Sensuously, like a warm hand, his gaze slid over her, causing her to shiver strangely. 'It would not be easy for a man to remain just good friends with a girl like you.'

Beth drew her long legs up beneath her on the sunbed and was half tempted to reach for her discarded sarong to protect herself further from that caress-like gaze. She looked back at him steadily. 'Yes, Giles and I are friends—but, as it happens, we are also related.'

'By blood?' He looked surprised.

'No, by marriage,' she informed him. 'My mother is married to his father.'

'I see. You have my sympathy.' He smiled a harsh smile. 'Have you had this cross to bear for very long?'

'If you mean, have we been stepbrother and sister for long? the answer is, only for just over four years.'

'So you were more or less an adult when it happened?'

'I was twenty,' she told him curtly. 'I don't know whether that made me an adult or not in your book.'

He smiled amusedly. 'Oh, I think you probably were. You have the look of a young woman who matured fairly early.'

And he had the look of a man who had been born mature. He was probably about thirty-five now, Beth guessed, but it was impossible to imagine him as a raw uncertain youth.

He flicked her a look. 'It must be a relief to you that you were spared the ordeal of having to grow up with him. That, I'm sure, would have been most unpleasant.'

'No more unpleasant than the ordeal your own brothers and sisters must have endured when they were growing up with you.' She had heard that he was the eldest of a numerous family. 'And they, of course, have the additional curse of having the same blood as yours in their veins.'

He smiled indulgently at her impudence. 'Believe me, that's not a curse, it's a blessing. The blood of the dei Cesaris is old and noble blood. Any man—or any woman—would be proud to have such blood flowing through their veins.'

Beth smiled a scathing smile, but she felt impressed all the same by the power of feeling that quivered behind his words. And she remembered what Giles had told her; that the dei Cesari family had been the most powerful family in the area for generations.

It was little wonder that this man behaved as arrogantly as he did. To him the assumption of power was as natural as breathing.

He asked her now, 'So, what brings you to Muretto? If I am not mistaken, this is your first visit here.'

He was not mistaken. 'Yes, it is.'

'Is it also your first visit to Italy?'

Beth shook her head. 'Not by any means.' Italy was a country she adored. She had visited it often and gained a smattering of its language. 'I've been to Rome and Florence and Venice——' she began.

'But never to Muretto,' he interrupted rudely. 'Never a few extra miles to visit your stepbrother. You were evidently not too keen to spend time with him, I fear. After all, he's been living here for over three years.'

'He travels a lot. He was never here when I was here.'

'And he's not here now,' dei Cesari pointedly reminded her. 'I take it that means that you're expecting him back?'

It was that question again. Beth's eyes narrowed suspiciously. Why was he so curious about Giles's movements? She looked at him unblinkingly. 'I'm sure he'll be back.'

'That sounds rather vague.'

Lord, he was persistent! 'He'll be back when he can make it,' she reiterated stubbornly. And when I can manage to track him down, she added silently to herself.

If only dei Cesari knew the reason for her vagueness! She was incapable of being any more precise!

He had leaned back a little on his stool and was eyeing her across the short distance that divided them. 'So, how long are you planning to spend at Muretto?'

As long as it took, was the honest answer. But she answered evasively, 'I'm not sure. A few weeks, perhaps. Maybe more...'

One black eyebrow lifted. 'You are fortunate indeed to be able to take so lengthy a holiday.' He scrutinised her with interest. 'Do you not work?'

'Yes, I work. I run my own business. So it's more or less up to me how much time I take time off.'

'That is most interesting.' He paused for a moment. 'What kind of business, if I may enquire?'

If I may enquire? That was a good one! From the word go he'd been quizzing her relentlessly. It was a little late now to start being polite about it!

Still, though she knew he was not really remotely interested, she couldn't resist answering with just a dash of pride, 'I run a picture-framing business with a friend—in London.'

'Just the two of you?'

'Yes, just the two of us.'

'And your friend doesn't mind you going off and leaving him? Or is he perhaps used to managing on his own?'

'My friend is a she, not a he!' Beth shot back at him, irked at the offensive tenor of his remark. 'And of course she doesn't mind my going off and leaving her, not when it's for——'

Just in time she managed to stop herself. She had been about to say 'for something as important as this', but she swiftly changed that to the equally true but less revealing, 'When I happen to be long overdue for a holiday.'

'And a holiday of indefinite duration. She must be very understanding, this friend of yours.'

Beth scowled across at him. 'She's got temporary help. I wouldn't have left her in a fix.' Then again she stopped short. Why was she explaining herself? Why should she feel accountable to him?

Perhaps it's become a habit, she told herself bitterly. Over the past few weeks, back in England, she'd spent endless hours trying to explain and account for herself. She pushed the thought from her mind. She would not dwell on that now. She had other more pressing problems to deal with.

Beth straightened her shoulders and regarded him squarely. 'Are you always so curious about other people's business?' Then, when he merely smiled an amused, mocking smile, she suggested, flicking back her almost-dry hair, 'I think it's time *you* answered some questions. You could start off by telling me what you're doing here.'

He shrugged his broad shoulders. 'I live here, *signorina*. As I told you already, I am a neighbour of yours.'

As he was quite well aware, that was not what she had been meaning. Beth clicked her tongue impatiently. 'So I believe. That is one of the less beguiling aspects of being here.'

He smiled sympathetically. 'Fortunately for both of us, we are not near neighbours. The Villa dei Cesari, where I live, is on the other side of the village.'

'That's a relief.' Beth looked back at him with feeling. 'I shall endeavour to confine my activities to this side of the village.'

'You have something to hide?'

Again she flared angrily, then managed to stop herself. He had this uncanny ability to put her

on the spot and she was absolutely determined
to reveal nothing of her business.

'I have nothing to hide,' she assure him calmly.
'I simply prefer to avoid unpleasant company.
Unlike you, Signor dei Cesari, I don't go looking
for trouble.'

'I'm pleased to hear it.' He shifted on his stool
and fixed her with a meaningful look. 'In that
case, I should have no trouble persuading you to
co-operate.'

'Co-operate?' she queried.

'Yes, co-operate, *signorina*. It was to enlist
your co-operation that I came here to find you.'

The way he said it sent a cold chill down Beth's
spine. On his lips, the word 'co-operation' had
an ominous ring. But she betrayed none of her
apprehension as she put to him, 'Tell me what
manner of co-operation you're looking for.'

He leaned towards her, dark eyes piercing
through her. 'Since you are unwilling or unable
to tell me when he'll be returning, I want you to
tell me where Giles is.' As she hesitated, he added
with a cruel twisted smile, 'You see, he and I have
some unfinished business.'

Unfinished business. That sounded even more
ominous! And Beth all at once felt thoroughly
pleased that she was genuinely unable to assist
him. She shrugged and looked coolly into the
dark eyes. 'I'm afraid I have no idea where he
is.'

'Are you saying that he left no forwarding address? You don't seriously expect me to believe that?'

'I'm afraid it's true. Ever so sorry.' Beth smiled across at him sarcastically. 'All I know is that he's travelling somewhere in Europe. It looks as though your business will just have to wait.' She turned away and rummaged in her beach-bag for her watch. 'And now, if that's all you wanted,' she informed him, glancing at it, 'I'd like to get back to the house and have some lunch.'

So saying, she began to gather up her things, stuffing them hurriedly into the beach-bag. She had already wasted too much time with this man. She should have made her exit sooner.

As she rose to her feet, he stood up also, and just for a moment Beth's heart beat uneasily. The look on his face was dark and dangerous. He clearly did not relish being shrugged off in this way.

But at least he made no move to stop her as Beth snatched up her sarong and tied it round her waist, then swung the beach-bag over her shoulder and bade him a curt and final, 'Goodbye.'

Instead, he simply stood and watched her. *'Arrivederci,'* he murmured beneath his breath.

Beth did not look back once as she hurried up the path that led to the garden and up to the villa, and with each step that widened the gap between them she could feel her inner tensions disperse.

By the time she had reached the villa she was feeling quite calm again, simply annoyed at herself for allowing him to upset her. Hadn't she had more than enough recently of trouble-making men? Hadn't she resolved, from now on, to steer a wide berth around all of them?

But at least, in the end, it had been relatively easy to get rid of him, she congratulated herself as she paused outside the back door to kick off her sandals and rub the sand from her feet. For the remainder of her stay here she'd be more careful to keep her distance.

She pushed open the door and stepped into the kitchen, the ceramic tiles deliciously cool against her feet. First, she would have a shower, then whip up some chicken and salad, with a glass or two of wine and some fresh fruit for afters. All that sun and swimming had worked up an appetite.

But she had just dumped the beach-bag by the kitchen table and was heading for the corridor that led to the bedroom when a soft click behind her made her swing around. At the sight that met her eyes, her heart flew to her throat.

Lorenzo dei Cesari was standing in the doorway, the look of an angry predator darkening his face.

'Let's start all over again,' he was saying as he stepped into the room and turned the key in the lock. With a harsh smile he dropped the key into his pocket. Then, soundlessly, he was closing the gap between them.

'I want you to tell me where Giles is—and I won't be leaving until you do.'

CHAPTER TWO

BETH backed away from Lorenzo, her jaw dropping in horror. 'What the devil do you think you're doing?' Struggling to disguise her anxiety as anger, she swung away furiously in an effort to escape him. But he snatched hold of her arm with fingers of steel and jerked her round roughly to face him again.

'*Signorina*, you are going nowhere! At least not until you have answered my question.' His voice was a deep and menacing growl—the blood-curdling growl of a lion incensed. 'I have given you one opportunity already. This, I warn you, will be your last!'

Beth struggled against him, knowing her resistance was futile. 'I've already told you I don't know where Giles is! Don't you think I would tell you if I did?'

In spite of her fear, there was a note of defiance in her voice that caused the black eyes to flash with impatience. 'No, *signorina*.' He gave her a rough shake. 'You do not, I'm afraid, strike me as the co-operative type. On the contrary, I suspect you take pleasure in thwarting me.'

Beth blinked a little at this uncannily shrewd judgement. If nothing else, he was a good judge of character. For the truth was that, even if she had known Giles's whereabouts, in spite of dei Cesari's heavy-handed persuasion, on principle she would have denied all knowledge.

Which meant, of course, that she was going to have a great deal of difficulty trying to convince him that she was telling him the truth!

She made another futile bid for freedom. 'Let me go! You have no right to do this!' But the fingers of steel around her arm simply tightened. He evidently felt that he had every right. But then, Beth decided, glaring impotently up at him, feeling as though she were caught in a vice, Lorenzo dei Cesari quite obviously believed that he had the right to do anything he wished!

He scowled down at her. 'Why bother struggling? Save your strength to tell me what I want to know.' Then, as she scowled back at him and tugged her arm rebelliously, he added, 'Besides, you have nowhere to run.' He patted the trouser pocket where he had slipped the backdoor key. 'You are in effect my prisoner now.'

Beth wrestled against him. 'Oh, no, I'm not!' Perhaps he had forgotten there was a front door, too!

But he had not forgotten, and, reading her mind, he informed her in a harsh tone, 'Forget that idea. There's no way you could out-sprint me to the front door—and it would only make me very angry if you were to try.'

He already looked sufficiently angry and, anyway, Beth knew he was right. She would be lucky to make it as far as the hallway if she were to try such a trick.

She glared at him in fury. 'What a bully you are! You barge in here, throwing your weight about as though I were a bunch of criminals instead of a lone, defenceless woman! How very impressive!' she taunted down her nose at him. 'You really are a very big man!'

He did not answer for a moment, just treated her to another of those caress-like looks, the black eyes removing stitch by stitch the still-damp swim-suit that she wore and the flimsy sarong at her waist, then pausing to savour without a flicker of shame the firm, soft, burning flesh beneath.

He raised one black eyebrow. 'Is that a challenge? Do you wish me to prove to you how big a man I am?'

Beth felt her heart jump. She had been incautious. To throw a challenge at a man like Lorenzo dei Cesari, especially a challenge so full of sexual innuendo, was really rather asking for trouble. Hastily she assured him, 'I meant nothing of the kind. I simply meant I'm surprised that you should go to all this trouble to try to force me to tell you something I've already told you I don't know.'

As he smiled without humour, the dark eyes glinting, for one nervous moment Beth was almost wishing that she did know where Giles was, after all. This man who held her prisoner was a law unto himself!

His eyes bored into her. 'I do not believe you and I am tired of waiting, *signorina*. Kindly do not waste any more of my time!'

She was getting nowhere. It was pointless to go on fighting him. Perhaps softer tactics might convince him. She must appeal to his better nature. If he had one.

She stopped struggling and deliberately dropped her voice. 'Signor dei Cesari, please be reasonable. Why would I not tell you if I knew? But I don't. All I know is that he's somewhere in Europe on business.' Her blue eyes implored him. 'Believe me, that's the truth.'

'The truth, *signorina*? Are you perfectly certain?'

Alas, there was no evidence of a better nature in the sharp tone of his response. As he ground the demand at her, he pulled her towards him so that in her suddenly unresisting state she stumbled a little and fell against him.

And in an instant all the fear inside her vanished to be replaced by a sensation that was vastly different.

The sudden hard warmth of him pressing against her was like a flame torch touching her senses. A flash of excitement, like raw electricity, shot through her body, making her blood leap.

Feeling suddenly breathless, her body limp against him, she raised her head. 'I wouldn't lie to you,' she told him.

'Oh, no, *signorina*?' He raised one black eyebrow. 'I do not believe you. After all, you are a woman.'

And a woman who was responding to the touch of a man as she had never responded before in her life. As he continued to hold her firmly against him, Beth made not the slightest move to resist him. It was as though his strength had drained all her strength out of her. If her life had depended on it, she could not have moved a muscle.

She looked into his face, her vision a little hazy. 'What do you mean, "you are a woman"?' she demanded helplessly.

'I mean, *signorina*, that lies and women go together like pasta and parmesan. Unfortunately, deceit is in their nature, especially when they are dealing with a man.' He paused for a moment and let his eyes roam over her. '*Signorina*, you are lying now.'

But she hadn't said a word—unless he was referring to Giles again. Beth shook her head. 'I promise you, I'm not.'

'Oh, yes, you are. And I can prove it.'

Beth frowned at him. 'Prove it? How?'

He smiled the smile of an amused alligator. 'Do you really want me to show you?'

Bewildered, Beth simply stared at him in silence. What she really wanted was for him to release her.

Again he smiled. 'Since you do not refuse my offer, *signorina*, it will be my pleasure to oblige.'

And then, before she knew what was happening, he was pressing her even harder against him. And she realised with a flash of horror, as he bent towards her, that he was about to kiss her.

His mouth was hard and hot and hungry, devouring her, making her gasp in outrage. Now it was he who had lost control of his senses! What the devil did he think he was doing?

She tried to pull away, but the hand that had held her arm was now pressing with easy strength against her back, forcing her semi-naked body more intimately against his, sending hot and cold shivers racing down her spine and a terror of panic clutching at her heart.

'Stop it this instant!' She was struggling like a maniac. 'I demand that you let me go at once!'

He leaned back a little and regarded her narrowly. '*Signorina*, I am simply doing as you bade. You asked me to prove to you that you were lying, and this is precisely what I am doing.'

The black eyes burned, but with contempt, not passion, as he jerked her to him once again, and proceeded to kiss her even more fiercely than before. His lips consumed her, prising her own lips open. She could feel the flickering heat of his tongue.

That was when Beth kicked him, hard, in the shin—though her bare-footed blow, she acknowledged with chagrin, probably hurt her more than it hurt him. If only she had been wearing a pair of steel-capped boots, she observed to herself with genuine regret as a pair of unrepentant black eyes smiled down tauntingly into her flushed face. He was evidently more amused than injured by her attack.

But at least she had achieved her principal objective, for he had released her, allowing her to step hurriedly away from him.

Beth regarded him furiously. 'What do you think you were doing? How dare you behave in such a manner with me?'

His smile merely widened. 'What's the matter, *signorina*? Did you not care for my method of proving that you are a liar?'

She had not cared for his method in the slightest. But even less did she comprehend what on earth he was talking about. Keeping her eyes fixed on him, as one might watch a snake, uncertain from which angle it might strike next, Beth demanded hotly, 'And what exactly did all that have to do with my supposedly being a liar? You've proved nothing, as far as I can see—unless it's that you have the manners and the breeding of an alley-cat.'

He was as immune to her insults as she had known he would be. The opinions of others, to Lorenzo dei Cesari, had no more value than a fistful of sand.

As he stuffed his hands into his trouser pockets and continued to regard her with that aloof, superior air, she added, 'Anyway, you couldn't possibly prove I was a liar. What I told you about Giles happens to be true.'

One black eyebrow arched at her. 'Frankly, I doubt it. However, that was not the lie that I have just disproved.' As the blue eyes narrowed, uncomprehending, he elaborated, watching her closely, 'The lie I refer to was not a spoken lie. It was the lie you were trying to tell me with your body.'

Beth flushed crimson, sudden shame overwhelming her. Had that moment of weakness, when his nearness had overwhelmed her, really been so blatantly obvious?

It would appear it had, as he went on to accuse her, 'Back there you were trying to tell me that you were available, pretending to offer me a trade-off if I would stop pressing you about Giles. It's an old female trick, but I should warn you, *signorina*, that I stopped falling for such tricks a very long time ago.' The black eyes burned into her for a long scathing moment. 'I know all about women who use their attractiveness to men to manipulate them into giving them what they want. And that is evidently the sort of woman you are. The very sort of woman that I despise most.'

Every last trace of crimson had drained from Beth's cheeks now. Her face as pale as chalk, she stood speechless for a moment. His accusations had a horribly familiar ring to them. They were almost word for word what Alec had told her. With an effort she managed to crush that hurtful memory and forced her tongue free from the roof of her mouth. 'That's a foul thing to say! I intended nothing of the sort! I don't go in for such female trickery. Whatever you thought I was offering, I'm afraid you imagined it!'

Still watching her, he nodded, his eyes dark with disbelief. 'Of course, *signorina*. I imagined everything. That's what you all say. Another female lie.'

'I haven't been lying to you—about anything!' Beth insisted, edging the conversation back to less personal ground. But, as he continued to look back at her with scornful dark eyes, she knew it would take more than repeated denials to convince him of the truth of what she was saying. Perhaps if she was to confide in him a little...

She sighed a long sigh, hating to make this concession. 'Look, Signor dei Cesari, the truth of the matter is that I've come here looking for Giles myself. I only wish I *did* know where he was!'

He regarded her narrowly. 'And why have you come looking for him?'

'His father's very ill. Possibly dying. My mother wants him to come back to England to see him.' That was part of the story, but only a part of it. There was no need for dei Cesari to know any more.

His eyes had grown curious. 'I'm sorry to hear it. But why couldn't you just have written to him, or phoned?'

'Believe me, my mother's tried. She wrote to him some weeks ago. She even sent him a couple of telegrams.' Beth bit her lip, remembering her mother's anguish. 'But she's had no answer, and when she phones he's never in. She asked me to come over here as a last resort.'

Dei Cesari shook his head. 'I don't understand it. You say your mother's been trying to contact him for weeks. I happen to know your step-brother was here less than two weeks ago.'

'Then I don't understand either.' Beth shook her head bewilderedly. 'He must have received my mother's letters. Why on earth wouldn't he have answered?'

'I'm the wrong person to ask.' Dei Cesari turned away. 'As you know, Giles and I are far from close.'

'Yes, I'm well aware of that.' Beth felt a flicker of annoyance. 'I understand that, for reasons best known to yourself, you've made a point of making his life difficult ever since he moved here.'

'Is that what he's told you? That I've made his life difficult?' He shot her a dark glance. 'I'm sincerely glad to hear it.' As she scowled disapprovingly, he turned round to face her. 'That, however, is beside the point for the moment. I'm curious to know how you intend to go about finding him.'

Beth shrugged uneasily. She had wondered that herself. 'He has friends here. Neighbours. Someone must know how I might be able to get in touch with him. I'm just going to have to go round and make enquiries.'

'I wish you luck.' Dei Cesari was scathing. 'I think you'll find that Giles has few friends in

Muretto. And the sort of people he consorts with are not the sort who are likely to be a great deal of help to you.'

'And what do you mean by that?'

He shrugged infuriatingly. 'I mean, *signorina*, that you're wasting your time. You may as well get on the first plane back to England.'

But she *couldn't* do that. She *had* to find Giles. She had promised her mother. Her mother was relying on her.

'On the other hand...' he glanced around him '...there must be plenty of clues right here in this house as to his likely whereabouts. Papers, letters, perhaps even a diary... These sorts of things can be very revealing.'

'Well, it wouldn't even cross my mind,' Beth assured him, 'to go rummaging among Giles's private papers! Maybe that's the sort of thing *you'd* do, but I happen to respect other people's privacy!'

'Good for you.' He was unimpressed. 'However, if you change your mind and happen to come across anything interesting, I'd be most grateful if you would keep me informed. As I told you, Giles and I have some unfinished business.'

He was the last one she would tell when she managed to track Giles down! Beth glared back at him with dislike as he leaned against the worktop, black eyes mocking her. As it was, she felt guilty about discussing Giles at all with him.

Her stepbrother, quite rightly, would be angry if he knew.

Poor Giles, she thought, having to put up with dei Cesari: he was the type who would take pleasure in making a misery of the lives of those to whom he took a dislike. And it would take little to antagonise a man like dei Cesari. Some unintentioned slight would be more than enough.

'For the moment I shall leave you.' He was glancing at his watch. Then on long strides he started to head for the door. He took the key from his pocket and turned it in the lock. 'Now you are free to leave whenever you choose.'

As he paused, Beth was watching him and the animal way he moved. Every action was imbued with the power and the grace—and the subtle menace—of a big cat on the prowl.

He turned arrogantly to face her and with a smile informed her, 'For myself, I prefer to leave by the front door.'

And it was in that very instant, as he came towards her, heading for the doorway that led to the front of the house, that a thought, like an illumination, flashed across Beth's brain.

Without thinking, she stepped in front of him, blocking his exit. 'You're behind Giles's disappearance, aren't you?' she accused, suddenly certain that she was right. 'He's gone off to get away from you. You've done something to him!' Her blue eyes sparked at him in outrage. 'Go on, admit it! Admit that I'm right!'

'I wish you were. I wish I had done something to him.' Dei Cesari smiled sadistically. 'I wish it with all my heart.'

Then his expression changed suddenly. His eyes seemed to darken. 'But you are keeping me, *signorina*. Please step aside. Unless it is your desire that I do something to *you*.'

It was quite clear what he was suggesting. Beth's stomach contracted. In her anger she hadn't realised just how close they were standing.

Cheeks aflame, she took a step sideways, suddenly more than happy to unblock his exit. One thing was for certain—she had no desire to suffer another of his punishing kisses!

'A wise decision.' He regarded her amusedly. 'I am, alas, at the moment a little pressed for time. Perhaps I can oblige you on some other occasion.'

'Kindly don't bother.' Her hostility crackled. 'The only way you could possibly oblige me would be by staying out of my life—and Giles's!'

'That would be my pleasure.' He grated the words at her. 'But unfortunately I cannot make you any promises until I have concluded my business with your stepbrother.' Then, with a cutting smile, he turned on his heel and marched swiftly past her and through the doorway. 'Goodbye, *signorina*. I wish you luck in your search.'

A moment later he was out in the hallway. Then she heard the front door open and close behind him.

'Damn you!' Beth's fingers were bunched into fists as she stared impotently for a moment at the spot where he had been. Then, on a sudden curious impulse, she hurried through to the front bedroom and stationed herself discreetly behind the net curtains. At the very least she owed herself the pleasure of seeing dei Cesari safely off the premises!

There was a long black Mercedes parked at the front door. He had evidently come looking for her at the villa before making his way down to the beach. She watched him climb into the driver's seat, cursing the dark profile as he slammed the door behind him then gunned the powerful engine and headed off down the drive.

I shall find out what you're up to, she promised herself fiercely as the Mercedes disappeared from sight. For suddenly she was certain that the link with dei Cesari was the link that could help her track down her stepbrother.

Dei Cesari might think he called all the shots, but he would soon discover he had another think coming!

Beth got down to work immediately.

After dei Cesari had gone she showered and had lunch, then sat out on the patio and started to make a list. First, she decided, she would tackle the neighbours. Perhaps one of them might be able to point her in the right direction.

She gazed around her at the well-kept little garden with its beds of bright fuschias and hedge of scented bay trees. This beautiful villa was one of half a dozen that lined this small corner of the Bay of Muretto. She felt a small pang of envy. Giles was so lucky to live here, a stone's throw away from the blue Mediterranean, less than two hours' drive from the capital, Rome.

A sigh escaped her as she turned back to her list. If only she knew a little more about her lucky, successful stepbrother her current task would be so much easier. But they had never been close, although she had often wished they could be. The truth was that she had only met Giles two or three times, and most of the bits and pieces she knew about his life—including all the horror stories about dei Cesari!—had come second- or third-hand to her from his father and her mother.

She knew he ran his own business and that it involved a lot of travelling, but she had never known precisely what he did. 'A little bit of this and a little bit of that,' was the beguilingly vague way that he had once described it, and Beth had never felt the need to press him further.

Now, however, she was wishing that she had, as she racked her brain for names to add to her list. Apart from the neighbours, who else did he mix with? Who were his friends? What clubs was he a member of?

She knew he wasn't sporty, so all the sports clubs were out. But there was a night-club that he had mentioned he liked to frequent. What was its name? Ronnie had spoken of it often. His son had taken him there when he had visited Muretto.

La Luna Verde! The Green Moon, she suddenly remembered, adding it hastily to her meagre list of names. Then another name came to her: he had an associate called Giacomo. She smiled with relief—her list was growing!

Beth sat back in her seat and gazed out towards the horizon, a pencil-thin line of deep cerulean blue. 'Don't worry, Mum,' she murmured with feeling. 'Whatever it takes, I'll find him for you!'

She felt a sharp clench of sadness as she thought of her mother and the terrible tragedy that was looming over her. It was so cruel that, after having already lost one husband—Beth's father had died, aged forty, in an accident—she was now having to prepare herself for the loss of another. The doctors had given Ronnie only a few months to live.

And, though that was bad enough, the situation was made worse by the fact that, because of some stupid legal mix-up about his house, if Ronnie should die before Giles could be contacted her mother would be left not only a widow, but homeless too. Giles's signature was needed to put the mix-up right.

It was Ronnie who had explained the situation to Beth and stressed the need for urgent action. 'The whole thing was cooked up to save my paying taxes. That's why Giles suggested putting the house in his name. But it was only supposed to be a temporary measure. Giles said it would revert back to me automatically, but the solicitor got it wrong.' Poor Ronnie had looked worried. 'I need Giles's signature for the house to be made mine again—so I can leave it to your mother.

'If I could I'd go to Europe to find him myself, but I barely have the strength to get out of bed. And your mother can't go. I need her here to nurse me. Would you go, Beth? Would you do us this favour?'

Beth had needed no persuading. Her mother had had more than enough sadness in her life. There was no way that Beth would risk letting her end up homeless.

And Giles would feel the same, she was absolutely certain. As soon as he knew about the legal blunder, he'd be more than anxious to sign.

That very afternoon Beth began her round of the neighbours. And though by evening she was replete with hospitality and cakes she was no further forward in tracking down Giles.

In the evening she took a taxi to La Luna Verde and spoke to the owner of the little night-club, but though he couldn't help her either he promised faithfully that he would contact Giacomo for her at the first opportunity.

'I can't give you his address or even his phone number,' he told her when she tried to weasel them out of him. 'He's a very private person. He would never forgive me. But don't worry—I'll let him know that you're looking for him.'

The following day Beth took time off to spend an hour on the beach, trying to figure out the link with dei Cesari, for the more she thought about it the more she felt certain that he was responsible for Giles's disappearance. If she could get to the bottom of what was going on between them, she was certain her task would be a great deal easier.

The only trouble was that she had never really known the nature of the hostility between Giles and dei Cesari. It was just a clash of personalities, as far as she could gather. Only now, it would appear, it had become a little more serious.

But then, as she lay there racking her brain, she was aware of a pair of eyes upon her.

She sat up and glanced around her. 'Who's there?' she demanded. Then an instant later she caught a glimpse of girl scurrying away between the palm trees that divided the beach from Giles's garden. 'Hey, who are you?' she called. But the girl had vanished.

She thought no more about it until she returned to the villa and discovered a note pushed under the back door. Curiously she opened it and read the message written there in an elaborately stylish feminine hand:

'Meet me at the Bar Italia in the main piazza at Saranno this afternoon at four o'clock. I'll be waiting at the table under the clock.' The message was signed enigmatically, 'M'—with a scribbled PS: 'It's concerning Giles and it's important.'

Beth instantly put two and two together. The note had obviously been left by that girl on the beach. And, though it was all just a little bit mysterious, this was one appointment she had no intention of missing. Cheering inwardly, she dug out a local road-map. This could be her very first break!

Saranno was a little inland village, about twelve kilometres from Muretto. Beth found it easily on the map. She had no trouble with the journey either, and at a quarter to four she was already parking the little car she had hired in a side-street just off the main piazza.

The sun was hot against the backs of her legs as she hurried across the cobbled piazza and headed for the Bar Italia. It was a typical alfresco Italian bar with rows of little tables with sparkling white table-cloths set out under big bright sun-umbrellas, the patrons, newly emerged from their afternoon siestas, drinking little cups of coffee or long cool drinks and unhurriedly watching the world go by.

Beth spotted the big clock right away. It hung above a rather more secluded table, partially obscured by a shoulder-high hedge. Her steps quickened a little with anticipation as she adjusted the collar of her blue striped shirt-dress and shook back her head of bright golden hair. Would 'M' be waiting for her? she wondered. And what on earth would she have to say?

Full of expectation, she headed for the hedge, a nervous smile of greeting forming on her lips. But as she came round to face the partially hidden table her smile shattered like a mirror stuck by a thunderbolt.

The figure who was waiting for her rose slightly in his chair, his black eyes mocking as they looked into her face.

'Well done, *signorina*. You are right on time. I knew I could rely on you not to let me down.'

CHAPTER THREE

BETH couldn't believe her eyes for a moment. What was going on? Was this some kind of trick? What the devil was Lorenzo dei Cesari doing here?

She swung away from him with a gesture of impatience. 'I may have come, but I'm sure as hell not staying! I'm so sorry to disappoint you, Signor dei Cesari!'

'No need to apologise, for I shall not be disappointed.' With the speed of a champagne cork bursting from a bottle his hand whipped out to catch her, mid-flight. 'For you will indeed be staying, *signorina*!' he assured her.

Once more those steel-wire fingers of his were curled unrelentingly around her fragile wrist. But this time the two of them were in a public place and Beth felt less totally at his mercy.

She did not struggle, she simply looked straight at him. 'Will you let me go, Signor dei Cesari, or shall I be forced to make a scene?'

'A scene, *signorina*? Why would you wish to make a scene? I merely wish to speak with you. What is wrong with that?'

'What is wrong with it is that I don't wish to speak with you! I thought I'd already made that perfectly clear!'

'Ah, but I insist.' His grip tightened a little. A look of pure intransigence settled across his face. 'I guarantee you will not be leaving this table until you have explained to me why you made that appointment with my sister.'

What appointment? What sister? 'What do you mean? I've never even met your sister!'

'Then how did it come about that you arranged to meet her here at this very table at four o'clock?'

Beth's brain was buzzing, trying to make sense of her confusion. 'You m-mean,' she stuttered, 'that "M" is your sister? That girl I saw...? The one who left me the note...?' She scowled down at him. 'How was I supposed to know?'

'What note? What are you talking about? Don't lie, *signorina*. I have already had enough of your lies.'

'And I've had enough of your accusations!' With a sudden burst of strength Beth snatched her hand away. 'The note said that I was to come here, that the person who wrote it wanted to see me about Giles!'

'More lies!' he taunted. 'Don't you ever tell the truth? You ought to try it some time. It might make your life a little easier.'

'And you ought to try believing me for once! It might make life considerably easier for both of us!'

It was at that very moment, as they glowered at one another, that a waiter arrived to take their order.

'Porta una birra.' Bring me a beer, Lorenzo instructed. Then he added in English, with a sharp glance in Beth's direction, 'Unfortunately, the young lady's not staying.'

'Oh, yes, I am!' Beth was suddenly curious. Why had dei Cesari's sister contacted her? And why was her brother here now in her place? And besides, it occurred to her, this might be the perfect opportunity to get to the bottom of what was going on between dei Cesari and Giles. She felt surer than ever that Lorenzo dei Cesari was the cause of Giles's disappearance. If she could understand why, she might be closer to finding him.

She turned to the waiter. 'Make that two beers. *Due birre.'* Then with an air of studied nonchalance she took the chair opposite Lorenzo. Perversely, now she had no intention of leaving.

Lorenzo's eyes were on her, his expression curious. 'Why this sudden turnaround?' he demanded. 'What stories are you planning to tell me now?'

'No stories,' Beth answered calmly, adjusting her dress over her knees. 'I was rather looking forward to hearing some explanations from you.'

He leaned back in his seat. 'No, you first, *signorina*. Explain to me why you contacted my sister.' As she started to shake her head, his eyes blazed with anger. 'Were you planning to give her some news about Giles? Or perhaps to pass on some secret message from him? How dare you?' he exploded. 'How dare you do such a thing? I absolutely forbid you to go near my sister!'

Beth forced herself to look back at him unflinchingly, though the force of his anger was like a physical blow. 'I haven't gone anywhere near your sister. As I already told you, it was she who approached me.' She reached into her bag, pulled out a slip of paper and tossed it across the table to him. 'That's your sister's note—if indeed "M" is your sister. As you can see, I wasn't lying,' she told him.

Without shifting his gaze he picked up the piece of paper, then scanned it quickly and tossed it back to her. 'You are right. This is without doubt my sister's writing.' He inclined his head and smiled a fleeting smile. 'It would appear that, at least this time, you were telling the truth.'

It was not exactly an abject apology, Beth thought wryly to herself. But then apologies of any kind were highly unlikely to be a part of this man's repertoire.

'*Due birre, signori!*' The waiter had returned to lay before them two glasses and two bottles of ice-cold beer.

Beth watched as Lorenzo reached for one of the bottles, poured it expertly and pushed it towards her. 'Thank you,' she murmured, and continued to watch him as he proceeded to repeat the operation with the other.

He was dressed in an ivory linen suit, with a plain blue shirt, open at the neck. And it suddenly struck Beth, as her eyes scanned his features, that, aside from being a remarkably powerful presence, he was also a remarkably attractive man.

Attractive, but dangerous, she reminded herself swiftly. For it was that don't-give-a-damn careless arrogance of his, which glittered from his eyes and tugged cynically at his mouth, that would remain forever the dominant quality of the man. Unwise would be the woman who ever got entangled with him!

He finished pouring and paused to take a mouthful of his drink. 'You said you saw my sister. Where did you see her?'

'Down at the beach. I just caught a glimpse of her. It was just before I went back and found the note at the villa.'

'And that's the only time you've seen her?' His tone was suspicious. 'You didn't by any chance approach her previous to that?'

'I keep telling you, I have never met your sister! Why do you persist in accusing me of lying?'

'Because you have yet to convince me that you are being scrupulously honest with me—about Giles, as well as in this matter with Mariella.'

So 'M' stood for Mariella, rather a lovely name, thought Beth. She looked back at Lorenzo. 'I would suggest that that's your problem. You know what they say about distrustful people— they're usually pretty untrustworthy themselves.'

'And you know what they say about people who avoid answering questions—they usually have something to hide.'

'And why should I answer your questions?'
Beth bridled. 'All you do is endlessly accuse me!
If you ask me, *you're* the one who's hiding
something!'

He had the grace to smile at that. 'And what
do you think I'm hiding?'

'I have no idea. But I intend to find out.'

'For what reason?'

'To help me find Giles.'

'You mean you really don't know where he is?'

Beth sighed with exasperation and picked up
her beer glass. 'How many times do I have to tell
you?' She turned away irritably and glanced
round the piazza, taking a long, slow mouthful
of her beer. This man was as persistent and as
maddening as a mosquito! It would give her
infinite pleasure to empty his beer over his head!

'I take it you met with little success in your
enquiries?' She could feel his eyes on her. 'I
warned you, didn't I?'

'Everyone I spoke to was incredibly helpful.'
Beth turned round to look at him as she
answered, ignoring the mocking look in his eyes.
'They just didn't happen to know where Giles is.
If they had known, I'm sure they would have told
me.'

'I hear you even went to La Luna Verde.'

'Have you been spying on me?' Her voice
flared with anger.

'Why would I spy on you?'

'That's not an answer! You see, *you*'re the one
who avoids answering questions all the time!

What's going on that I don't know about? You're hiding something, aren't you? Admit it!'

He leaned back in his seat and smiled at her infuriatingly. 'You know, you really are quite beautiful when you get angry. Your colour rises in the most flattering way.' He allowed his smile to broaden wickedly. 'I must try to think of ways to keep you angry.'

'I'm sure you won't find that difficult. It seems to come naturally. You're the most infuriating man I've ever encountered!'

He laughed at that, a low earthy sound that momentarily broke the tension between them. Then his black eyes narrowed and his expression grew hard again. 'Joking apart, allow me to warn you, *signorina*, that you have seen only a tiny sample of how infuriating I can be.'

'Is that some kind of warning?'

'Take it as you want to. Consider it more of an insight than a warning, if you wish.'

Insight or warning, the information was superfluous. Beth already had him marked down in her mind as a man capable of inflicting infinite irritation.

'I'll say one thing,' she told him, her blue eyes cool and steady, and her colour—she hoped!— returned to normal, 'you certainly live up to your reputation. Every bad thing I ever heard about you appears to be true.'

He merely shrugged, an arrogant gesture. 'I'm sure what you heard is only the tip of the iceberg.

As I have told you before, your source is unreliable.'

Which brought the subject neatly back to Giles again. Beth toyed with her beer glass and glanced across at him. 'I know you're not much good at answering questions, but perhaps you might have a go at this one?' she suggested with some sarcasm. She paused for an instant, then put to him evenly, 'What do you reckon your sister was referring to when she said in her note that she wanted to see me about Giles?'

Something flickered momentarily at the back of his eyes and his tone was impatient as he answered, 'How on earth would I know? You would have to ask my sister.'

So he did know! She was sure of it! Beth continued to stare across at him. 'Was there something going on between Giles and your sister?' The idea had come to her like a light-bulb flashing in her head.

He did not answer immediately. Instead he picked up his beer glass. '"Going on?"' he repeated finally, lacing the words with distaste.

So her revelation had been right! 'Yes, going on,' she persisted. 'Were Giles and Mariella perhaps having an affair?'

Lorenzo laid down his glass with a loud thud on the table-top. Suddenly there was a storm brewing at the back of his eyes. 'Perhaps you are unaware that in this part of the world to call the honour of a young woman into question is a very serious charge indeed.'

All he was doing was convincing her further, yet Beth could see it would be wise to tread carefully now. 'I meant no disrespect. I simply wondered if that might be the link between Mariella and my stepbrother.'

He looked back at her in silence, then turned away abruptly and let out a violent oath in Italian. The black brows drew together and his tone was crushed pebbles as he informed her now in a carefully lowered voice, 'Your stepbrother, *signorina*, has a great deal to answer for. Not content with all his other philandering, for a bit of additional carnal amusement he seduced my sister and turned her into a whore!'

He paused for a moment to snatch a breath before continuing, and his eyes were like thunderbolts starting from his head. 'This stepbrother of yours has sullied my sister, and he has done it virtually under my very nose, while she was in my care, staying with me for the summer. He has totally ruined an innocent young girl—and, worse, he has dishonoured my family name!'

As he came to the end of his fearsome diatribe, it would not have surprised Beth had she looked round to discover the piazza where they were sitting reduced to a pile of rubble. He had vented his fury with the power of an earthquake. The ground beneath them seemed to tremble.

And yet she could not quite bring herself to accept that Giles deserved such a spectacular show of condemnation. 'Surely,' she ventured, with more daring than diplomacy, 'any relationship your sister may have entered into with Giles was entered into of her own free will? I don't see why you have to portray her as Giles's victim.'

'You're suggesting that she isn't?' The demand cracked like a whip. 'Perhaps you assume that all young people adhere to the same moral standards as your stepbrother?'

Beth blanched a little at the ferocity of his accusation, but forced herself to answer evenly, 'I'm afraid I know nothing of the standards Giles adheres to, so I'm really in no position to judge.'

Her calmness only enraged him further. 'Perhaps you approve of his behaviour? Perhaps you adhere to the same moral standards yourself?'

But now it was Beth's turn to be angry. She stiffened in her seat and regarded him steadily. 'Signor dei Cesari, as I have already told you, I know nothing about my stepbrother's private life—but I deeply resent the implication of that remark!' She took a deep breath to calm the outrage sweeping through her. 'In fact, I demand that you retract it immediately!'

With a veiled expression in those mysterious dark eyes of his, Lorenzo dei Cesari looked into her pale face with its hectic spots of colour over the cheekbones and in a low voice offered, 'You are right, of course. I should not have said that. I allowed my anger to get the better of me.'

As though to placate her, he reached for her beer bottle and emptied the remainder of its contents into her glass. Then he pushed the glass towards her with a small smile. 'Drink. It will help to calm your nerves.'

Beth almost smiled at the sheer black gall of him. So he *was* capable of a dignified apology, after all—and, laced with that charm of his, it was quite irresistible. She had swallowed it as easily as a spoonful of molasses!

He was emptying the remains of his own beer bottle into his glass as he told her now, 'Perhaps I was also wrong to accept my sister's word that it was you who set up this meeting, not she. After all, I know how distraught she has been over the past couple of weeks since Giles's disappearance. It's quite likely, I suppose, that she arranged to meet you in the hope that you might be able to put her in touch with him.'

'In that case, she would have been wasting her time,' Beth wasted no time in reminding him. 'As I have already assured you on numerous occasions, I am quite unaware of Giles's whereabouts.'

The dark head nodded. 'Indeed,' he acknowledged—though it was impossible to tell whether he actually now believed her. But at least he refrained from dwelling on the issue and instead put to her, his tone sympathetic, 'My sister has been quite distraught since Giles abandoned her.'

Beth frowned a little. 'What makes you think he's abandoned her?'

'Oh, he's abandoned her. There's no doubt about that. After he'd taken what he wanted of her he dumped her quite unceremoniously.' He drew in breath and held it for a moment, and Beth could sense the monumental effort he was having to make to keep his bubbling anger in check.

Then a moment later he continued, 'Of course, all of this I have only learned recently. A matter of days ago to be precise. In desperation, my sister opened up her heart to me and begged me to find Giles and bring him back to her.' The dark eyes grew shuttered. 'I'll bring him back to her! Preferably in pieces the size of a postage stamp!'

As he sat back in his seat and drained his beer glass, Beth found herself watching him with a sense of dawning comprehension. Right from the start of this conversation, when he had first brought up the subject of Giles and his sister, she had almost heard the sound of pieces falling together.

'Now I understand! This is a personal vendetta!' There was a bite in her voice. Her eyes were censorious. 'That's what the inquisition on the beach was all about! That's why you burst in on me at the villa! You're desperate to find Giles so you can tear him to pieces in order to avenge your sister's tarnished honour!' She laughed a scathing laugh. 'Don't you think such behaviour is just a little out of place in the final decade of the twentieth century?'

'I suppose you would think so.' He laid down his empty glass. 'I suppose you do not believe a girl's honour is worth defending.'

He was wrong about that! If he but knew it, Beth's own honour was something she had always defended with vigour. But that didn't mean she agreed with dei Cesari!

'I don't necessarily believe your sister's honour has been tarnished. You say Giles simply used her, but I have no proof of that. Perhaps he loves her—have you ever thought of that? Perhaps he never meant to leave her at all. Perhaps this whole thing is simply a misunderstanding.'

'Some misunderstanding! He disappeared without a word.'

'But he's bound to be back, sooner or later. After all, this is his home. So, instead of jumping to conclusions and making all sorts of melo-dramatic threats, why don't you just wait until he returns and then talk the whole thing over in a civilised manner?'

'How very British. But that's not my way. I prefer to tear him apart first, and then talk things over afterwards.'

The observation was delivered with a venomous scowl that sent an icy shiver crawling down Beth's back. Poor Giles, she thought again. One thing was for sure: he had definitely picked the wrong man's sister to get involved with. No wonder he was keeping out of dei Cesari's way!

That was it! She did a mental double-take.
Suddenly she had her answer. That was why Giles
had disappeared!

She leaned across the table. 'You threatened
him, didn't you, when you found out what was
going on between him and your sister? That's why
he's disappeared. That's why I can't get hold of
him!'

'There was no need for me to threaten him.'
A smile twisted around his lips. 'He must have
known before he laid a hand on my sister what
I would do to him when I found out.'

'What a bully you are! You must really have
scared him to make him take to his heels like
that!'

'It wasn't I who made him take to his heels. I
didn't know what was going on until after he'd
gone.'

Beth didn't believe that for a moment. It was
just a ploy to put her off the track. Then a sudden
thought occurred to her. 'Is your sister pregnant?
Is that the reason for all this fuss?'

'No, my sister isn't pregnant.' The words fell
like a sledge-hammer. 'Believe me, if she were
there would be no place far enough away for that
bastard of your stepbrother to hide. I would track
him down if he'd gone to Outer Mongolia!'

Beth had no doubt of it. She felt relief on
Giles's behalf. 'Then why has he gone—if not
because of you?'

'I have no idea.'

But his eyes flickered as he said it. She knew it was a lie. 'You're just trying to cover up. You don't want to admit that you threatened him with violence.' She peered into his face, her hostility luminous. 'What are you hoping to get out of this, anyway? Are you hoping he'll decide to stay away for good?'

'That would suit me very nicely.' His jaw snapped like a steel trap. 'And, though she can't see it at the moment, it would be best for Mariella, too.'

'But what about me? It wouldn't be best for me! And it wouldn't be best for my mother and Giles's father!' Suddenly her voice was breaking with anguish. 'If I can't find him, it'll all be your fault! When my mother's been left homeless, you'll be the one to blame!'

Dei Cesari instantly picked up her lapse. 'What's this about your mother being left homeless? You never mentioned such a thing before.'

And she hadn't meant to now. 'I don't wish to discuss it. I need to get Giles to agree to sign some highly important documents. They have to be signed before his father dies or the consequences will be very serious.' She glanced away, a little angry at herself for divulging such private family business. 'It's not necessary for you to know any more than that.'

'OK, I understand. And I appreciate your concern.' Dei Cesari's eyes had softened a little as he leaned across the table towards her. 'I don't know exactly what your situation is, but our objectives appear to be similar. Both of us want to find Giles as quickly as possible, so wouldn't it make sense for the two of us to work together?'

'So you can tear him into pieces the size of a postage stamp? No, thanks, I don't think I care to assist you in that objective!'

'Don't be so melodramatic. I have no intention of laying a hand on him.'

'He didn't think that or he wouldn't have disappeared! Why on earth should I believe you?'

'Because I swear it's true.' Lorenzo sighed deeply. 'Look, I'm not at liberty to tell you what they are, but my reasons for wanting to track Giles down are just as urgent as yours. Let's work on this together. Let's co-operate.'

'Do you take me for a fool?' Beth glared across at him. 'You've already told me what your reasons are. You've already admitted it's some stupid vendetta! Do you really think I would cooperate with you when all you're interested in is harming my stepbrother?' Suddenly her limbs were trembling with anger. 'You really like playing the big boss, don't you? You really enjoy screwing up other people's lives.'

'Only some people's lives.' His eyes were unblinking. 'Only the lives of those who deserve it.'

'Such as Giles, for example?'

'Precisely. Such as Giles. People who make a hobby—no, a career—out of screwing up other, innocent lives.'

Beth could not accept that. 'That's a wild exaggeration! You can hardly accuse Giles of screwing up your sister's life simply because he got romantically involved with her.'

He paused before answering and then he told her, 'It is not only my sister's life that Giles may have ruined. Many others have fallen victim to him, too.' His eyes were on her. 'He has to be stopped. Before he ruins the lives of many more.'

Beth scoffed at that. 'You're making a mountain out of nothing! And, anyway, what do you care about what he might do to others?'

'I care.'

'I doubt it! It doubt you even care about your sister! All you care about is avenging the name dei Cesari!'

'And you, *signorina*, appear to care about nothing. Don't you believe people have a duty towards one another?'

'Of course I believe that! Why else do you think I'm here, trying to find Giles before his father dies?' As a flicker of something crossed his eyes—regret? Compassion? She could not decipher it—she leaned towards him urgently and pleaded, 'Only you can help me. You must drop your vendetta. You must let Giles know that he has nothing to fear by coming out of hiding and coming back here. There must be *some* way of letting him know...' Her voice broke with desperation. 'Please! You've got to help me!'

'It would do no good. Take my word for it. And anyway, as I've already told you, it's not because of me that Giles has run away.'

'I don't believe you! You just don't want to help me! All you're interested in is doing things your way and making sure you get your pound of flesh! What sort of man are you? Don't you care about anyone? I keep telling you it's essential that I find Giles!'

She was aware that her voice had risen hysterically and that her heart was suddenly clamouring in her chest. She could feel her breath tight in her throat and the blood beating like a tom-tom in her veins.

And she could not stop herself. Her frustration was unbearable. Tears of desperation were smarting in her eyes. 'Please take back the threats you've made! Do it for me! Do it for Ronnie and my mother!'

'I can't, Beth. Believe me, it's something I can't do.' His expression earnest, he reached out towards her, as though to take her hand in his.

But she would not be placated by this serpent! Furiously Beth snatched her hand away from him. 'You bastard!' she seethed. 'You rotten bastard! How can you do this to innocent people?'

Then with a final harsh glance at him she swung out of her seat—straight into the path of one of the waiters, who was making his way between the crowded tables.

There was a spectacular crash as his tray and its contents made shattering contact with the cobblestones, and the entire clientele of the Bar Italia paused in their refreshments to witness the scene.

Though her limbs were shivering with emotion, her blood pounding so violently that she thought she must faint, with towering aplomb Beth turned to the waiter. 'I'm terribly sorry. *La prego di scusarmi.*'

Then, like a woman on a tightrope, without a glance to left or right, she was striding across the piazza, making her escape.

CHAPTER FOUR

BETH fled from Saranno and out into the countryside, driving without knowing where she was going, just following whichever road took her fancy.

'Damned pig-headed man!' She felt like screaming and giving vent to all her bottled-up frustration. He was even worse than Alec, she thought with helpless fury. Trying to reason with him was like trying to draw blood from a stone!

She scarcely noticed the unfolding countryside—the soft rolling hills peaked with deep green cypresses, and the shimmering silvery olive groves that flanked her. All she knew were the thoughts that swarmed inside her head.

That episode at the café had brought back so many memories of another time, just a few weeks ago, when she had felt equally as helpless and unfairly victimised. Only that time the man involved had been Alec.

She could see him in her mind's eye, berating her in fury. 'You conniving bitch! You just wanted to use me! All you were ever after was my money!'

'You're wrong! You're wrong!' How fiercely she had protested. 'It wasn't like that. I swear it, Alec!'

But nothing she could say had managed to convince him. 'If it wasn't for me, you'd be nothing!' he'd accused her. 'And just take a look at the thanks I get!'

It was true, she thought bitterly: she owed Alec a lot. If it hadn't been for Alec's generosity she would never have had the funds to start her picture-framing business. And how had she thanked him? she asked herself brutally. She had thanked him by breaking off their engagement just a matter of weeks before they were due to be married.

No wonder he had said the things he had said to her. No wonder he had been resentful and hurt and angry. But he was wrong, all the same. She had never meant to use him.

She stamped on the brake as she rounded a corner just a little too fast, and nearly skidded. All at once the road had become like a corkscrew as it turned and twisted up the hillside. And suddenly she could smell the tangy scent of the countryside. She rolled down the window and drank it in gratefully.

At the top of the hill she drew the car to a halt and sat staring down at the view spread out before her—the tumbling hillside, the red roofs of Saranno, and off in the distance the blue splash of the Mediterranean.

Somehow she had survived those awful weeks with Alec, when it had seemed he had turned the whole world against her. And she had emerged from the ordeal with a sense that she had grown stronger. If she could cope with that, she could cope with anything.

She sighed to herself. That was easily said. She hadn't reckoned on crossing swords with Lorenzo!

With sudden impatience she climbed out of the car and gazed at the sunlit panorama all around her, for the first time taking in its beauty. And in that instant her spirits lifted.

She clenched her fists and raised her face to the sky. She would come through this too, whatever happened. She would not let Lorenzo dei Cesari beat her!

'Excuse me, *signorina*. May I talk with you?'

It was the following day and Beth was down on the beach, stretched out on her stomach on the sunbed, snatching a relaxing half-hour before lunch.

She rolled over and squinted up at the intruder, shading her eyes from the sun with one hand. Then a moment later she sat up abruptly. 'You're Mariella, aren't you?' she queried.

The young woman nodded. 'Yes. And you must be Beth.'

She was dressed in white trousers and a bright red top, with shoulder-length hair, as dark and glossy as her brother's, and the same air of total self-assurance.

She smiled down at Beth. 'I've come to apologise for getting you into trouble yesterday. I'd no idea Lorenzo would keep our appointment for me. I couldn't come myself. He'd locked me in my room.'

Beth looked up at her in horror. 'You mean he locked you in your room when he found out you were supposed to be meeting me?'

The girl nodded. 'He was absolutely furious. That's why I told him the meeting was your idea.'

And he would be equally furious, it occurred to Beth, if he knew what his sister was up to now! She pulled a face and glanced around her as she swung her legs round to sit facing Mariella. 'Let's just hope he hasn't followed you, or we could both end up being locked in our rooms!'

'Don't worry, he's not here. He's in Rome for the day.' Mariella smiled and hesitated for a moment. 'Do you mind if I join you for a couple of minutes?'

'Absolutely not! Make yourself comfortable.' Beth shifted along the sunbed to make room.

'It's OK, I'll sit here.' With a composed little smile Mariella seated herself cross-legged on the sand. She took a deep breath. 'It's about Giles,' she began. 'You've got to help me to get in touch with him.'

Beth sighed and shook her head. 'I wish I could. I'm rather anxious to get in touch with him myself.'

'But you must have some idea where he is! He's your stepbrother! He must have told you something!' As she spoke the young girl's fingers fidgeted with the sand, the first sign she'd given that she was less composed than she seemed. 'Is he in Zurich? He often goes there.'

Beth pounced immediately. 'You think he's in Switzerland? Where does he usually stay when he goes there?'

Mariella named a hotel. 'But I've already tried calling. I was told he wasn't there.' She shook her head, her eyes filling with tears. 'Oh, how awful! You were my last hope!'

With a stab of sympathy Beth leaned towards her, all at once seeing behind the mask of self-assurance a desperately unhappy little girl. 'Don't be upset. He hasn't gone forever.'

'I wish I could believe that.' Tears spilled down Mariella's cheeks. 'But even if he does come back, he won't want to see me. He doesn't love me any more.'

'Don't be silly,' Beth chided gently, anxious to soothe the girl's evident pain. She reached out and touched Mariella's arm softly. 'He's bound to come back, I absolutely promise you, and when he does I'll insist that he sees you.'

Mariella choked back a sob. 'Thank you. That's kind of you.' Then she wiped away her tears and pulled herself together. 'The trouble is Lorenzo doesn't understand. I know he's trying to find Giles, but only so that he can punish him. He's told me he'll never let me see him again.'

Beth pursed her lips. 'He's a hard man, your brother. I can't say I envy you being his sister.'

'He's not as bad as he seems. You've probably just seen the worst of him. Most of the time he's a wonderful brother.' To Beth's surprise Mariella defended him instantly. And there was a sudden fierce pride in her voice as she added, 'The trouble is he expects everyone to be as strong as he is. You'd never catch him blubbing if he was in my situation. He'd just shrug it off and get on with his life again.'

Beth didn't doubt it for a second. Few things, she sensed, would throw Lorenzo dei Cesari, and certainly nothing so trivial as love for some woman.

'I doubt he knows what it is to be in your situation,' she answered with a hint of condemnation. 'Somehow, I can't see him giving his heart to anyone.'

'Oh, but you're wrong! You don't know about Caterina. Caterina broke his heart.'

Beth's eyebrows shot disbelievingly up her forehead. Tell me about it! her expression was saying. And, happily, Mariella obliged.

'The two of them were engaged for years and Lorenzo was absolutely devoted to her. She was an orphan, you see, and she relied on him for everything, and he looked after her as though she were a child. He was so incredibly generous to her—and she didn't deserve it. Just when they were on the point of getting married, she left him and ran off with another man.'

As Mariella said what sounded like a rude word in Italian, Beth found herself suddenly understanding something. This contempt Lorenzo had for manipulative women appeared to be rooted in bitter experience. She grimaced inwardly as it occurred to her also that, on the surface, she and Caterina had much in common.

'But Lorenzo, being Lorenzo,' Mariella continued, 'just carried straight on as though nothing had happened. It must have hurt him terribly, but he never showed it.' She paused for a moment and stared at the sand. 'Sometimes I think he never really got over it, though, for that was nearly two years ago now and there's never been another serious woman in his life. Maybe he's still secretly in love with Caterina, or maybe he doesn't believe in love any more.'

She sighed, then raised her eyes apologetically. 'But here I am babbling on about Lorenzo and I've already taken up enough of your time.' Smiling at Beth, she scrambled to her feet. 'Thanks for listening to me. I feel a little better.'

'I'm glad to hear it,' Beth smiled encouragingly. 'I'm sure that everything will come out right in the end.'

It *has* to, she thought with a surge of determination. For herself and her mother, as well as for Mariella!

But by the evening, despite having made several more enquiries, Beth was still no further forward.

Feeling a little dispirited, she showered quickly and slipped on a cool, loose, green-flowered caftan. I'll treat myself to a martini before dinner, she decided. Maybe that'll cheer me up!

At Giles's well-stocked bar in the sitting-room Beth fixed her drink with plenty of ice in it, then stepped through the french windows on to the patio, paused for a moment to gaze up at the stars and sank with a sigh into one of the wicker armchairs.

She took a sip of her drink and closed her eyes for a moment, letting the balmy night air fold deliciously around her, listening to the chirrup of the crickets in the garden and the soft distant murmur of the sea.

And already Beth was starting to feel a little better. In spite of everything, this place was sheer heaven!

But the very next instant there was a sharp crack behind her, like a dry twig snapping underfoot. Then, even as she whirled round, momentarily startled, a male voice bade her, '*Signorina, buona sera.* I was hoping to find you here.'

In an instant heaven was transformed into purgatory!

Beth sprang to her feet. 'What do you want? You have no right to come barging in here!'

From the way he was leaning casually against the low wall that bounded the patio, a tall dark figure in white trousers and black shirt, it appeared that, contrary to Beth's opinion, he believed he had every right to be there. But, then, Lorenzo dei Cesari, Beth pondered with irritation, would lean equally proprietorially against the portals of heaven. He would believe it was his right to be anywhere he chose!

No doubt that was why he ignored her admonishment and, as was his habit, went straight into the attack.

'Where is my sister?' he demanded harshly, his tone making the words more of a threat than a question. 'I happen to know she was with you this afternoon. I would like you to tell me where she is now.'

Beth laid her drink on the cane table beside her and deliberately took her time about answering him. 'Since you're so well informed about your sister's movements, I'm surprised you have to turn to me to discover where she is now. What's the matter? Did your spies let you down? Well, that's your problem. I'm afraid I can't help you.'

Then with careful aplomb, she turned away from him and reseated herself disdainfully in her chair.

She knew that that would not be the end of it, of course. Men like dei Cesari, as bothersome as horse-flies, unfortunately did not simply disappear. Still, the gesture pleased her, for she sensed it had irked him, and irking dei Cesari was becoming one of life's small pleasures.

She picked up her drink as he stepped on to the patio and raised it to her lips as he strode over to face her. 'I warned you I did not want you to speak with my sister. I thought I'd made that perfectly clear.'

The moonlight that dappled the broad black-clad shoulders sent flashes of quicksilver dancing through his hair—hair as glossy as a beaver's back and, as always, pushed back carelessly from his strong-boned face.

And again, with a tightening in the pit of her stomach, Beth silently acknowledged the sheer beauty of the man. It was almost a tragedy that one so physically blessed should possess such an ugly and overbearing nature.

Beth swallowed her drink. 'Perhaps you should also have made it clear to your sister that you don't wish us to meet. As before, it was Mariella who approached me.'

At least he did not bother to argue with that. 'What did she come about? Giles, I expect.' He fixed her with a look of accusation. 'And what did you tell her? Did you tell her where he is? Is that where she's gone now? Has she gone to find him?'

The man was obsessed! 'Giles, Giles, Giles! Is Giles all you ever think of?' Beth demanded hotly.

'Fortunately, no.' His eyes snapped across at her, as he took one of the cane chairs and seated himself opposite her. 'To fill one's mind constantly with a thought so unpleasant is something only a masochist would do.'

'And you're not a masochist?'

'Definitely not.'

'I tend to agree. Sadism's more in your line.'

Lorenzo smiled, unperturbed by her gibe, and leaned back a little in his chair. He laced his fingers across his chest and fixed her with a penetrating eye. 'So tell me what passed between yourself and my sister.'

'I'll tell you nothing! It's none of your business. Anyway, I'm not in the habit of divulging private conversations.'

He moved then, making her muscles tense within her, half afraid he might grab hold of her and drag her from her seat. But instead he simply shifted his own chair a little closer, so that there was barely a foot between them.

'My sister is seventeen years old,' he told her, the black eyes piercing into her like bayonets. 'In spite of appearances, she's little more than a child and children do not have private conversations.' He regarded her grimly, with growing impatience. 'So kindly just tell me exactly what you spoke about.'

Beth narrowed her eyes at him, condemning his arrogance. 'At seventeen years old she's scarcely a child—and anyway, how old does one have to be to have a private conversation? You really are most incredibly presumptuous! Why don't you ask your sister what we talked about?'

'Because she's not here. I've already told you that. And, don't worry, just as soon as you've told me where she is I shall talk to her at considerable length.'

What a bully he was! He was quite insufferable. Suddenly, Beth's heart went out to

Mariella. No wonder the girl had sought refuge with Giles. At least Giles would have treated her like an adult!

She turned on Lorenzo now with indignation. 'Why don't you leave the poor girl alone? Let her live her own life and work out her own problems. I'm sure she doesn't need you interfering!'

He regarded her harshly. 'Interfering, you call it? Anyone with a degree of responsibility in their make-up would realise that what I'm doing is trying to protect her.'

'If you ask me, it's you she needs protecting from! No wonder the poor girl's run away!'

'So, she's run away. You appear to know that much. Perhaps you would now do me the favour of telling me where to?'

'I don't know where to. I was merely surmising. I was simply saying I wouldn't blame her for trying to escape from you.'

'You think it is good that she's gone off after that degenerate, that she's gone chasing that amoral stepbrother of yours?' He paused for a moment in his demolition of Giles's character and suggested with venom in his voice, 'Perhaps this was something you encouraged her to do?'

There he was again, making personal attacks on her, casting up accusations that were miles from the truth! Beth glowered across at him. 'To be perfectly honest, I don't really know whether it would be a good thing or not if she's gone running after him, as you say. Unlike you, I don't have the habit of leaping to conclusions until I've listened to all sides of the story.' Her blue eyes flashed. 'I've heard your side of the story and, to some extent, I've heard your sister's, but I haven't heard yet what Giles has to say.'

'So, you defend him?'

'I have no reason not to. He's done nothing really wrong, as far as I know!'

Lorenzo sat back in his seat and surveyed her, a thoughtful expression on his face. 'You're a hard girl to persuade,' he observed in a light tone. 'Are you always this stubborn about everything, I wonder?'

'And do you accuse everyone who knows their own mind of being stubborn?' Beth shot back at him.

He smiled at that. 'You've got an answer for everything. I believe you could talk your way out of the line of a firing squad.'

It had been meant as a sort of compliment and part of her acknowledged that. But another, guilty part of her instantly recalled that Alec, just a week ago, had made a similar comment—and that that had definitely been intended as an insult.

Instead of shrugging good-naturedly, as she would have done normally, she shifted her gaze away from Lorenzo. 'Why don't you mind your own damned business and stop passing judgement on me?' she snapped.

He seemed to study her for a moment. Then, to her surprise, he challenged, 'Why are you so damned touchy all the time? The least little criticism and you almost explode.'

Colour washed her face. Was she really that bad? Was she starting to get neurotic?

She kept her eyes fixed on the palm trees at the bottom of the garden as she endeavoured to respond lightly, 'Isn't everyone like that? I'm sure no one particularly enjoys being criticised.'

To her relief, he did not pursue the subject. 'You're also a pretty rotten hostess. I've been sitting here for a good five minutes and you haven't even offered me a drink.'

Beth spun round to face him. 'You've got a nerve! Why on earth should I offer you a drink? You seem to be forgetting, I didn't invite you here!'

'No; it was my idea.' He smiled amusedly. 'I dropped in to bestow upon you an unexpected pleasure. Aren't you grateful?' The black eyes twinkled.

'Sorry to disappoint you, but no, I'm not!'

'That's too bad.' He shook his head sadly. 'But I'll have a drink anyway. Just give me what you're having.'

That was the last thing she intended doing! Beth sat back stubbornly in her chair. 'I'd really prefer it if you just left now.'

To her surprise he stood up. This must be a miracle! But, instead of heading back across the patio, he strode purposefully towards the french doors. 'Are the drinks in here?' he enquired over his shoulder. 'Since you're so inhospitable, I'll have to help myself.'

A moment later he had disappeared into the sitting-room, and Beth heard the clink of glasses and bottles as he made himself busy at the bar.

She jumped to her feet and strode to the open doorway. 'What do you think you're doing?' she demanded hotly. 'This is Giles's house! You have no business in here.'

'I can't find the ice.' He was immune to her outrage. 'Where do you keep it? In the kitchen?'

'No, it's not in the kitchen, it's in that dispenser!' With a gasp of frustration, Beth stepped into the room. 'I'll get it for you,' she snapped, heading towards him. If she didn't take charge of this situation instantly, the wretched man would go marauding all over the villa! 'Give me your glass!' She almost snatched it from him, then stepped in front of him to press a button on the ice dispenser. Two perfect ice cubes clunked into the glass. 'Now, what do you want to drink?' Her eyes scanned the row of bottles.

'I told you; I'll have what you're having,' he answered. And there was the hint of an irritating smile in his voice. He evidently found the situation amusing.

Beth poured a tiny measure of gin over the ice cubes, then added an equally tiny measure of vermouth. She thrust the glass back to him, deliberately ungracious. 'There's your martini,' she told him flintily. Unless he had the sensitivity of a wart-hog he ought to get the message that she would rather he didn't linger!

'Still angry, I see.' He was smiling down at her—and she had contrived to trap herself between him and the drinks-table. He took a mouthful of his drink and looked down at his prisoner. 'Now where were we...? Yes, you were about to tell me why it is that you're so sensitive to criticism.'

'I was about to do no such thing!' She jostled against him uselessly. 'Now kindly move! You're blocking my way.'

'So, who's been criticising you, sweet Signorina Beth, to make you so defensive all the time? Your family, perhaps?'

'No, not my family!'

'Friends?'

'Perhaps.'

'A boyfriend, maybe?'

'It doesn't matter who it was! It's none of your damned business!' And inwardly she cursed for betraying herself so easily. 'Stop quizzing me all the time and just get out of my way!'

Needless to say, he simply moved closer. Beth could suddenly feel the virile potent heat of him.

'I think it was your boyfriend. You do have a boyfriend?' The dark eyes looked down at her. He reached out to touch her hair.

'Not any more.' Beth's heart had almost stopped beating. She felt the world disappear at the contact with his skin. And, as she looked into his face, she was so overcome with confusion that she had to remind herself to keep breathing.

'They must have been serious, then, these criticisms of his.' Lorenzo smiled a cloudy smile and stroked her cheek with the backs of his fingers. 'Tell me, sweet Beth, what did you do to make the poor man so angry with you?'

She could have said nothing. It would have been wiser. But Beth found herself saying, 'I broke off our engagement.'

His fingers paused for a moment in their caressing. 'I see,' he murmured. Then he smiled softly. 'Is this a practice you make a habit of?'

Beth swallowed. 'Of course not.' She could scarcely speak. With each touch of his fingers her heart pounded within her. She took a deep breath. 'Let me go,' she murmured, though she knew he would not and that, in truth, she did not want him to.

He laid down his drink and slipped an arm round her waist, then looked into her face for a long, long moment. He shook his head slowly. 'No, *cara*,' he answered.

Then he was drawing her closer, pressing her against him, and longing, like a knife, went lancing through her, as the warmth of his body seemed to engulf her.

It was that formidable power in him, drawing her like a magnet. She could not have resisted it even if she had wanted to.

The touch of his lips was like an explosion, a fire-cracker bursting over her senses. As she parted her lips eagerly his tongue invaded her, her own tongue flicking in eager response.

For, suddenly, to deny this fierce hunger he stirred in her seemed like a false and pointless exercise. She had never experienced a reaction like this before. The wildness he awoke in her was irresistible, intoxicating.

As his hand possessed her breast, naked beneath the thin caftan, suddenly her arms were flung about his neck. Her fingers knotted in his hair, adoring the thick, soft, silky feel of it. And all the while her lips pressed against his. She could not get enough of his kisses.

His hand circled her breast, strumming the hard peak of it, lighting vivid new sensations deep in her loins. Then she heard him moan softly as she pressed against him, feeling his arousal hard against her hips. And it struck her that never before in her life had she felt so physically free with a man.

A moment later, his breathing husky, he drew away and looked down at her with smouldering dark eyes. 'Whatever complaints he had, this boyfriend of yours, they can't have been that you're an unresponsive lover. You're a regular little volcano, aren't you?'

Beth winced at that and stiffened resentfully. He had made her sound like a bitch in heat. And the truth was that she had never kissed Alec in this way—not Alec, nor any other man.

And suddenly, more than anything, she longed to demolish his belief that her passion had been genuine.

She leaned against him and switched on a false smile. 'Will you do me a favour, just one little favour? Will you do as I asked and drop your vendetta against Giles?'

He reacted precisely as she had known he would. 'So, that's what it was all about!' He pushed her away from him. 'Another of your little trade-offs. I might have known!'

To her surprise, the words stung in spite of the fact that it was she who had virtually put them into his mouth. But she managed to hide that as she responded harshly, 'Why else would I allow you to kiss me like that? You didn't seriously think that I enjoyed it?'

He cursed in Italian and swung away from her. 'Well, you're wasting your time. I won't be dropping my vendetta, not even if you try crawling into my bed!'

He paused at the french doors and snarled across his shoulder, 'Don't think you can do to me what you did to your boyfriend! I'm sure before you cast him aside you managed to extract from him everything you wanted.'

His eyes raked her pale face. 'You treat sex like a commodity, something to be coldly traded for favours. And that, *cara* Beth, is the behaviour of a whore!'

The words hit her like a spray of broken glass. Beth recoiled visibly. How dared he insult her? And, as the anger boiled inside her, she was suddenly filled with an overwhelming desire to hit back at him.

He would not get away with it! She could play dirty, too! As he started to stride across the patio, she stepped forward quickly and addressed his retreating back.

'No wonder your fiancée walked out on you!' she spat. 'Who could bear to be married to a man like you? I imagine that every day of her life she must put up thanks for her lucky escape!'

He did not deign to retaliate with words, but, as she stood there, quivering with anger and triumph, knowing she had touched him on his one raw spot, he turned to fix her with a terrible look.

The next instant he was gone, melted into the shadows, leaving her with a sudden illogical desire to run after him and take back every word she'd just said.

For already she regretted her vindictive little outburst. And she would soon live, she sensed, to regret it even more.

CHAPTER FIVE

A THOUSAND times over the next twenty-four hours Beth wished she'd run after Lorenzo and apologised. Her outburst, though provoked, had been mean and contemptible. She felt deeply and bitterly ashamed of herself.

She slept badly that night, endlessly tossing and turning, her brain besieged by a pack of cruel demons.

Lorenzo's accusation that she was shallow and manipulative, though she knew it to be mistaken, had affected her deeply—far more deeply somehow than Alec's similar accusations. And knowing that was so disturbed her even more.

Why, in spite of the fact that she detested him, did dei Cesari wield this uncanny, destructive power over her?

But that question was merely one of many. She easily found good reason to push it aside. For far more pressing was the dilemma of what she should do about Mariella.

Yesterday evening when Lorenzo had confronted her she had refused to co-operate purely on principle. But that principle, she now realised, had been of shaky validity—for she had been assuming that his interests and hers were in conflict, and in this particular instance that simply wasn't so.

Though she barely knew the girl, she cared about Mariella. The last thing she wanted was for her to come to some harm. And in spite of the heavy-handed way he sometimes treated his sister, Beth was certain that Lorenzo cared deeply for Mariella, too. Unlikely as it seemed, just for once she and Lorenzo shared a common goal—namely that no harm should come to Mariella and that, as quickly as possible, she should be found.

And yet Beth had deliberately stood in the way of that goal by insisting that she had no idea where Mariella might be. For, though it was perfectly true that she did not know for certain, there was one possibility that sprang immediately to mind.

Zurich.

Had Mariella gone to Zurich to try to find Giles? Was she wandering around Switzerland at this very minute? It was definitely a possibility one ought to consider.

I should have told her brother, Beth acknowledged to herself. It was wrong to keep that information from him. In her current deeply vulnerable state, who knew what danger Mariella might be in? The thought of the distraught, impulsive teenager wandering alone around Europe gave her goose-pimples.

There was only one thing to do. She had to tell Lorenzo.

First thing next morning she phoned the Villa de Cesari. 'He's gone to Rome and won't be back until evening,' she was told. Then, when she phoned again just before dinner, the number was constantly engaged.

I'll go there in person, she decided reluctantly, and if he's not there I'll leave a note. For there was no way she could let another night go by without passing on such vital information.

She dressed quickly in a denim sun-dress and a pair of strappy sandals, and headed in her hired car for the village. Outside a busy bar she paused to ask directions, then ten minutes later she was driving through the main gates of the elegant, imposing Villa dei Cesari, high on its hill over-looking the village.

Her stomach clenched as she headed up the driveway, between cypress trees ranked like a guard of honour, till she came at last to the front of the villa. She parked neatly and climbed out, then hurried up the stone steps that led to a huge wood-panelled front door.

An old-fashioned brass bell invited her to pull it. She did, a trifle nervously, and stood back, waiting.

But no one came to answer her ring. She pulled the bell again, and then she tried knocking.

'Damnation!' she muttered as she listened in vain for the sound of approaching footsteps on the other side of the door. 'Perhaps there's nobody at home. Perhaps I shall be forced to leave a note, after all!'

But there were lights on all over the house. There must be someone in! Perhaps there was another door round the back of the villa.

Her sandalled feet crunching against the gravel, she proceeded to make her way round the back, the long trek making her all too conscious of just how vast the villa was. Set amid glorious gardens, moon-dappled now, it was quite as big as some English castles. Lorenzo and Mariella, its only residents apart from servants, must rattle about inside it like loose coins in a pocket.

She passed tennis courts, a huge lake with swans and ducks and water-lilies, and stretches of glorious, sweet-scented flower-beds. And then, all at once, she rounded a corner and saw before her a gleaming swimming-pool.

The next instant, even as she paused to admire it, the mirror-like surface was suddenly shattered as a dark shape came hurtling down from no-where and pierced the blue water as straight as an arrow.

Beth gasped at the suddenness of the appar-ition. It was as though a thunderbolt had shot down from heaven! But then she was aware of a moving shadow beneath the dimly lit surface of the water. A second or so later the shadow sur-faced, paused for an instant to shake its dark head, then struck out in an effortless crawl. What she had seen was no thunderbolt from heaven— it had simply been Lorenzo dei Cesari diving from the high board into his pool.

She hurried to the edge of the pool and called out, 'Signor dei Cesari, if you don't mind, I'd like a moment of your time.'

At once he turned and a strange slow smile curled around the wide, well-shaped lips. 'What a pleasant surprise. You've come to join me. So, what are you waiting for? Come on! Jump in!'

At least, for once, he hadn't leapt straight for her jugular! It appeared that this evening he was in a more equable mood.

Ever hopeful, Beth smiled down at him. 'I must decline your invitation. I just stopped by to tell you something that suddenly occurred to me. It's about Mariella. I think I know where she might be.'

'Is that a fact?' He was swimming towards her, then lifting himself up a little from the water to rest his arms on the edge of the pool. 'Why don't you come in and tell me all about it?'

'I don't think so. As you can see, I'm not exactly dressed for swimming.' Beth felt a flicker of irritation. Was he going to be difficult, after all? She looked him in the eye. 'I really think it would be better if you were to come out of the water and join me here.'

'You think so, do you?'

'Well, it would be a bit more civilised than trying to conduct a conversation with you down there and me up here.'

'You could be right.' His eyes flickered with amusement, as though he was enjoying a private joke. 'Well, if that's what you consider to be the civilised thing, I'm only too happy to oblige.'

He flashed up a smile at her, then with a shake of his dark head proceeded to lift himself effortlessly out of the water. And suddenly Beth knew what the private joke had been, for he was standing before her without a stitch to his name.

As she blinked with embarrassment, he made no effort to cover himself. And, after all, why should he? He had no reason to be ashamed, for he was beautifully built. Every proud masculine inch of him was a veritable pleasure to behold.

Only Beth was doing her best to confine her beholding to that area of his anatomy above the level of her eyes. She cursed herself inwardly. How utterly naïve she was! She might have known that the wretched man would take perverse pleasure in springing something like this on her!

'You were saying...? About Mariella? Please continue.' He was still standing there, quite unashamedly, before her, as though he regularly conducted his business in the nude.

Then, to her huge relief, before she could answer he was brushing past her to one of the pool-side chairs where a large yellow towel was lying folded. In one deft movement he had flicked the towel round him, securing it lightly around his lean hips. He dropped into the chair and stretched his long legs in front of him. 'What's the matter?' he enquired. 'Have you suddenly lost your tongue?'

Beth glared at him. He was enjoying her discomfort. 'Not at all,' she shot back at him, hastily regaining her composure. 'It's just that my attention was momentarily diverted. With such rare entertainments thrust so unexpectedly before me, I temporarily lost the thread of my story.'

Lorenzo smiled at her dry humour. 'One can scarcely blame you, *signorina*. Entertainments of so rare a quality are not something a girl can enjoy every day.'

He leaned back in his seat, black eyes twinkling, and, in spite of herself, Beth smiled in response. 'Who said I enjoyed it?' she parried.

For a moment their eyes met and meshed together, and an unexpected flash of empathy passed between them. For one brief golden instant they were a man and a woman bonded together by a mutual attraction. A powerful attraction, both spiritual and physical, that transcended all the previous barriers between them.

Then the moment passed and Beth was aware of a strange sinking feeling deep within her. A feeling of anticlimax and disappointment. She had wanted that moment to last forever.

Lorenzo was nodding towards the chair alongside him, inviting her to take a seat. 'You were saying, *signorina*?' he prompted. 'You think you know where my sister is?'

'It's only an idea. I don't know for certain. I want to be quite clear about that, Signor dei Cesari.'

He paused for a moment. 'Let's drop the formalities. I think, in the circumstances, you may call me Lorenzo. After all, I call you Beth.' He smiled, then continued, 'About Mariella...I am most interested to hear this idea of yours.'

Beth took the chair next to him and proceeded to recount the reasons why she suspected his sister might have gone to Zurich. 'Personally, I think it's unlikely that she'll find him there—that's why I didn't follow it up myself. But she seemed so upset, capable of anything, that I couldn't help wondering if maybe she'd gone there.' She ended her tale with a self-conscious little shrug. 'At any rate, I thought you ought to know.'

'That was very responsible of you.' He was watching her closely. 'I shall make some enquiries first thing tomorrow.' Then he leaned towards her, his eyes narrowing at her curiously. 'So, what prompted this sudden change of heart?'

'What sudden change of heart?' She feigned incomprehension. A discussion of the volatile emotions he aroused in her was the very last thing she wished to embark on. It was not even as though she understood them herself. But, as he was about to insist, she decided to appease him with as bland an explanation as she could come up with.

'Last night I was angry with you. I didn't want to help you. But, later, I realised that that was wrong of me. I shouldn't have allowed my anger against you to get in the way of Mariella's welfare. It would be terrible if anything was to happen to her.' She paused, aware of the black eyes on her, and dropped her own gaze now as she added, 'While I'm at it, I may as well apologise for my rudeness. I said certain things to you last night that I had no business saying.'

There was a silence, broken only by the chorus of the crickets and Beth found herself wondering if she had said too much. Then Lorenzo spoke. 'Why were you angry with me? What had I done to incur your wrath?'

Beth's eyes snapped up at that. She burst out laughing—the incredulous laughter of disbelief. 'Why was I angry with you? You must be crazy! Don't you know you've done nothing but bug me and insult me since the very first moment I set foot in Muretto?'

He had sat back in his chair, so that his face was in shadow. 'In what way did I insult you, *signorina*?'

'You've accused me of being a manipulating woman.' She struggled to keep the sudden hurt from her tone. 'The kind of woman you tell me you most despise.'

'You are right; I do.'

'Well, I'm not like that.'

'Are you sure, *signorina*?'

'Absolutely sure.'

'What about this boyfriend of yours? Did you not manipulate him—then discard him when he was of no further use to you?'

'Of course I didn't! I was fond of Alec. And it was he who offered me the money to start my business. It wasn't I who asked for it!' She should never have said it. It just popped out. Beth turned away miserably. 'It's not what it sounds like. I didn't agree to marry Alec because of the money and then run out on him after I'd got it.' She stopped in her tracks. She was just making things worse by voicing the accusations that Alec had hurled at her.

She shook her head. 'It's a long, complicated story and I'm sure you have no desire to hear it.' She bit her lip. 'And I don't want to tell it. I've had more than enough of it over the past few weeks.'

As a silence fell, she turned away awkwardly. 'Look, I think it's time I went back home. I've told you what I came to tell you.'

But before she could move, Lorenzo suddenly spoke. 'Why did you break off your engagement?'

Beth turned to look at him. 'I discovered I didn't love him.' There was no point in trying to fudge the truth.

'Did you ever love him?'

'At first I thought I did.'

'But after a while you simply grew tired of him?' There was an edge to his voice. 'How very convenient.'

'It wasn't like that. I didn't just grow tired of him.'

Even as she started once more to defend herself, she wondered why she was bothering to do it. Why should it trouble her that Lorenzo thought badly of her? Why was she so anxious to put him straight?

But she carried on, 'The trouble was I never really knew Alec well. He works in the Middle East—he's a quantity surveyor—and I only ever saw him for a few weeks at a time when he came home on leave every year. I thought it was love, but then I realised that I wasn't looking forward to his leaves any more. I tried to feel differently, but somehow I couldn't. I just knew it would be madness to go ahead and marry him.'

As his eyes held hers, she could see in their depths that he was remembering Caterina. She expected a withdrawal, but instead he told her, 'Alas, it happens. Sometimes we fool ourselves. And, even when it's real, love dies all too frequently. Unfortunately, it is something we have to learn to live with.'

How had Mariella described him at the time of his heartbreak? 'It must have hurt him terribly, but he never showed it... He just carried straight on as though nothing had happened.'

Beth now understood exactly what she had meant. There was no hint of sorrow in the words he had just spoken, though Beth thought she had caught the faintest echo of bitterness lurking behind his philosophical words. Even now, she sensed, there was anger deep within him for the faithless betrayal of the woman he had loved.

Beth looked into his face and felt a sense of sorrow that his bitter experience had marked him so profoundly. What a terrible loss it was to the world that a man like Lorenzo, a man of deep, instinctive passions, had apparently turned his back on the possibility of love.

His eyes were on her, making her gaze drop away, as she wondered if he could read what she was thinking. Such crazy thoughts! Where had they sprung from? Hurriedly she chased them from her head.

But if he had read into her mind, he was saying nothing, as, all at once, he rose to stand before her. 'So, *cara mia* Beth, now that we've got that straight, I think I shall resume my swim.'

His hand was on the towel as though he might remove it, making the hairs prickle uncomfortably on the back of her neck. Beth jumped to her feet. 'Of course. I'll leave you. I didn't mean to interrupt.'

But all at once his free hand was on her shoulder, halting her progress as she was about to dart past him. 'I was rather hoping that you might join me. Wouldn't you care for a nice cool swim?'

Yes and no. It was humid and sticky and the still blue pool looked exceedingly inviting. But a frolic in the nude with Lorenzo dei Cesari was not something she had any particular desire for. The very thought made her stomach clench most peculiarly. A mere symptom of her distaste, she told herself firmly.

But even as she started to shake her head, the corners of his wide mouth were dimpling with amusement. 'Don't worry, you can borrow one of Mariella's costumes. There are several over there in one of the changing-rooms. And I'll get myself some trunks to spare your blushes.' He adjusted the towel and smiled down at her. 'I usually only swim in the nude when I'm alone, and this evening I wasn't expecting company.'

With a firm hand he was guiding her towards the changing-rooms, taking her agreement as already given. And Beth could really see no cause for objection. After all, what would she do if she went back to the villa? She would just sit on her own and read a book. And the prospect of a swim here in this luxurious pool was really rather tempting.

Even the thought of Lorenzo's company, for once, did not repel her. On the contrary, he seemed perfectly palatable tonight.

She chose a deep turquoise swim-suit, flatteringly cut, from the haphazard pile she found lying in the changing-room. It was a trifle tight, which was scarcely surprising. Mariella was a skinny little thing.

'I like a woman who fills her swim-suit,' Lorenzo remarked from his perch on the topmost diving-board when she finally emerged. He let his gaze trail over the smooth curve of her hips, the dip of her waist, the full thrust of her breasts. 'I swear that costume has never looked so good.'

Beth blushed a little, appreciating the compliment, for the forthright sincerity of it was reflected in his face. Delicately she lowered herself into the water, swallowing back the compliment that rose to her own lips. For now that he was respectably clad—in a hip-hugging pair of dark blue swimming-trunks—she had dared to examine his physique more carefully, and there was no doubt that he, too, was eminently worthy of applause.

With his powerful broad shoulders and muscular chest, his hard flat stomach and long powerful legs, he possessed a masculine beauty that could make one's heart leap. Which was why she said nothing and refrained from watching him as he executed a neat back-flip into the pool.

She did not like this effect he sometimes had on her. She really did not like it at all.

But the swimming was good and the pool was magical, set as it was in this strange enchanted garden. As Beth swam on her back, gazing at the stars, the sky seemed like a canopy of midnight-blue velvet, the moon a crescent of palest silver dangling from an invisible thread.

She sighed and allowed her limbs to relax, letting her body float like a cork. And suddenly all her worldly troubles seemed miles away, part of a totally different universe.

The next second a shrill shriek rent the silence, causing her to bob upright and glance anxiously around her. 'What the devil was that?' she spluttered.

'That was only Lavindra, one of the peacocks. She sometimes gets quite vocal at this time of night.'

'Lavindra, the peacock! How very exotic! She almost made me jump out of my skin!' Beth smiled across at him, then, as she looked closer, her smile turned into a curious frown. 'Good gracious, you've been busy!' She laughed, swimming towards him. 'Where did all this stuff come from?'

He was sitting on the edge of the pool, his long legs dangling in the water, while at his side was arranged an assortment of low tables, each laid out with dishes of tasty-looking titbits. And, standing in a bucket of ice at his shoulder, a bottle of the very best champagne.

'I arranged for it to be brought while you were changing. Come and join me,' he invited. 'There's far too much here for one.'

He was right about that! There was enough for an army—platters of *crostini*, stuffed red peppers and wild mushrooms and pizza dripping with mozarella cheese. There were fat green olives, figs and tiny pastries and a bowl piled high with peaches and grapes.

'Surely you don't expect us to get through all of that?' Beth was laughing as she climbed out of the water. This totally spontaneous, extravagant gesture was somehow typical of the man, and in a funny sort of way she found it endearing. She took the ice-cold champagne flute he was holding out to her and watched as he eased the cork from the Dom Perignon.

'Stop complaining,' he teased her as she sat down beside him and he splashed some of the sparkling liquid into her glass. 'I'll bet you haven't had a proper meal since you came here. Here's your chance to make up for lost time.'

'Here's my chance to get fat, you mean!' Beth quipped in response, swallowing back an exquisite mouthful of the champagne. 'As you already observed, this swim-suit of your sister's is quite tight enough on me as it is!' She refrained from adding that she would be in danger of bursting out of it, if she were to consume anything even approaching half of this magnificent spread. Somehow, she had the feeling that he had already thought of that himself!

Yet, in spite of her resolve to exercise restraint in the face of such satanic temptation, an hour later she had done eminent justice to the culinary skills of the dei Cesari kitchen staff. She wiped her lips on a white linen napkin and shook her head firmly at Lorenzo, as he pushed towards her yet one more pastry.

'Absolutely not!' she protested. 'I couldn't manage another thing. You have it,' she told him, pushing the plate back towards him. 'I'm sure you have room for just one more.'

'I'm already about half a dozen ahead of you. Still, if you insist, I shall make this small sacrifice.' He popped the pastry into his mouth and winked at her. 'Absolutely delicious!' he decreed.

'How do you do it?' Beth was laughing. 'You eat more than any man I've ever seen, and yet there isn't an ounce of fat on you.' She reached across and laid her hand on his stomach. 'Look at you! Not a spare centimetre! All of you is solid muscle!'

She had touched him without thinking. She had not meant to appear intimate. It was simply that the atmosphere between them was so relaxed that the gesture had come quite naturally. But at once she regretted it. She felt his stomach muscles harden and saw a dark cloudy look come into his eyes.

'Forgive me,' she apologised, immediately feeling awkward, and starting to snatch her hand away. But already he had caught it, holding it firm and flat against him, and the warmth of him was suddenly scorching through her fingertips.

'Forgive you for what?' Now he had moved closer. One hard-muscled thigh was pressed against her own. And Beth had no more resistance than a straw hat in a hurricane, as his arm circled her shoulder and he drew her towards him.

There was a moment of silence and total stillness, as though the earth had frozen on its axis. Then he was leaning to kiss her, his hands moving to touch her, and all at once there was a thunder in her brain.

This is it, this is it, Beth was thinking numbly, not at all certain of what she was meaning. All she knew was that she was powerless to stop what was beginning, and that even had she had the power she would not have used it.

For it was as though some dark force had decided her fate for her and now she was reaching out blindly to embrace it.

CHAPTER SIX

LORENZO'S lips were like molten fire against Beth's, sending darts of hot pleasure coursing through her. All at once it was as though a torch had ignited her. Her entire being seemed to burst into flames.

He kissed as he did everything else in life—with a power and a passion that took one's breath away. Yet he revealed, too, the skill and sensitivity of one for whom making love was an art.

There was nothing hurried or coarse in the embrace that now seemed to devour Beth and melt her very bones. And that intense, yet gentle quality of his kisses was what made them so powerfully irresistible.

Not that Beth, at that moment, was capable of such analysis. Her brain seemed to have dissolved into a fog of sensual wonder. Like her limbs, it no longer seemed answerable to its owner. There was only one thing of which she was capable at that moment, and that one thing was total surrender.

Yet there was nothing passive or weak in that surrender, for at that moment his will and her own were fused together. What she seemed to be surrendering to was not Lorenzo, but her destiny—and the overpowering passions that he aroused within her.

It was quite unique, the way he made her feel. No man's kiss before had made her blood leap. Nor had she ever, in all her innocence, dreamed that the naked touch of flesh against flesh could whip one's senses into such a state of sweet ecstasy.

'Beth, mio amore! Cara mia Beth!'

The voice that spoke her name was thick with the desire in him. 'Lorenzo!' she responded, her own voice a weak croak. And suddenly the sound of that name on her lips was the sweetest sound she had ever heard.

He had drawn her hard against him. His arms were tight around her, his hands moving, caressing, driving her wild. And her own arms were twined just as hungrily around his neck, her fingertips trembling as they caressed the dark hair. It felt like silk, she acknowledged wonderingly, heavy and soft and lustrous and cool. She longed to bury her face against it and kiss it, and breathe in the sweet, rich scent of it, as though breathing in the essence of the man himself. For he was like a drug, an intoxication. Her senses simply could not have enough of him.

He had drawn her back against the pool's tiled perimeter, cushioning her shoulders with his arm, and the more his hard torso crushed down upon her, the more longingly she pressed into him. The weight of him against her was a tantalising

pleasure. A foretaste of more intim
to come.

With his lips he dropped kisses on her face and
her shoulders, with his free hand pushed back
the tangled blonde hair, and where his lips
touched her skin burned like a volcano, sensation
upon sensation erupting within her.

His hand was moving down to caress her
shoulder, his touch gentle, urgent, firm and sure.
Then, as it moved to caress the soft swell of her
breast, Beth knew that this was what she had been
waiting for.

The breath caught in her throat as his fingers
made contact with the firm, throbbing flesh,
grown hard with desire, his hand sliding beneath
the thin fabric of her swim-suit to cup the aching
orb in his palm. He moved now to the other
breast, moulding it lovingly, bruising the
burgeoning nipple with his fingertips, making her
jaw clench tightly as a shiver went through her,
as sharp and as vivid as an electric current.

Then, in a gesture that reflected her own rising
excitement, with an impatient hand he was
tugging at her swim-suit, peeling away the top,
like the skin from a peach, to expose her eager
upturned breasts.

A dart of sheer carnality went shooting through
her, lighting a fire like Vesuvius in her loins.

'Kiss me!' she begged him from deep in her
throat. 'Kiss me, Lorenzo! Oh, please, please kiss
me!'

had no need of her
dark head was bending
could feel his warm breath
. She tensed in anticipation,
head back as his lips, firm and
around her burning flesh.

ce pleasure went jolting through her,
so to , so vivid it must be a sin—though, if she
had died at that moment, quite without question
she would have left the world a happy and unrepentant sinner.

In echoing spasms of delight, as her whole
body shivered her fingers clutched and tugged
wildly at his hair. And she could scarcely bear
him to continue—or worse, bear him to stop—
as his teeth gently grazed her sensitive flesh,
inflicting an almost unbearable pleasure.

Then he was raising his head and drawing
himself up to look at her. 'Now the other one,'
he told her. 'We must not make her feel neglected.
She must have her share of kisses, too.' He kissed
her mouth with wet lips and smiled a smoky smile
at her. Then before she could protest, had she
really wanted to, he was slithering down again to
repeat his sweet torment, this time on her other
breast.

She wanted to cry, 'Stop!' or 'Don't stop,
ever!' All at once both seemed to mean the same
thing. For the fine line between longing and
needing had evaporated. What she longed for was
no longer within her power to deny herself, and

her need for him was as vital now as her need to breathe air.

As her body arched against him, proclaiming her hunger, she felt his hand slide down to her half-discarded costume, easing it over her un-resisting hips. Then, a moment later, he was tossing it away from her, leaving her ripe and naked under his gaze.

He admired her quite openly. *'Come ti desidero!'* And his hand swept over her, ur-gently, lingeringly, smoothing the curve of her belly, the soft bloom of her thighs. 'Never have I desired a woman so much.'

She did not doubt his words as he wriggled from his swimming trunks and pressed against her, rampant and hard. And she just sighed and clung to him all the more hungrily as he slipped a folded yellow towel beneath her hips.

Then he was drawing himself on top of her, easing apart her thighs, and her heart was pounding with anticipation, her blood thun-dering like an avalanche in her veins.

His hands covering her breasts, he kissed her gently, though there was a fire behind that gentleness that flickered dangerously. It was a gentleness that could not even begin to camou-flage the force of a passion just barely controlled.

Then his mouth, and his hips, were moving with more urgency, as though his body could not wait to possess her now. And, just as her own anguish grew to be almost unbearable, his tongue thrust forcefully between her lips and, in one parallel movement of his hard hips, their two hungry bodies were suddenly one.

Beth cried out, 'Oh, my darling!'

And her cry was echoed.

'Adorata mia!'

Then there were no more words and no more need for them, as their bodies expressed with wordless eloquence the soaring spiritual closeness, the fears, the hopes, the passions, that flow between a man and a woman engaged in that most intimate and universal of rituals, as old and as constantly renewed as time.

It was a lifetime later that Beth blinked her eyes open and found herself still lying in his arms.

Lorenzo kissed her. 'How beautiful you are. The most beautiful woman in the world.'

She had not been sleeping, nor even dozing, really. She seemed to have been floating, high above the world. Even now, as she blinked at him, she felt strangely separate, as though she were gazing down on herself from a cloud.

She said in a detached voice, frowning slightly, 'I don't know how that happened. Nothing like that has ever happened to me before.'

Lorenzo smiled lazily and took her hand in his, then, delicately, one by one, began to kiss the tips of her fingers. 'Nothing quite like it has ever happened to me, either. I think both of us were taken a little unawares.' Then, as her frown merely deepened, he added more seriously, 'You have nothing to fear. Let me make that quite clear. Considering the risks of the days we live in, perhaps I should have assured you of that a little earlier.'

Beth dropped her eyes away, understanding. 'You have nothing to fear, either,' she reassured him—and she could feel him smile softly as he stroked her hair.

'Yes, I know that. You were—inexperienced. Perhaps that is also something you ought to have told me.'

Beth flushed a little. Yes, she was inexperienced. The few fumbling attempts at sexual gratification that she had engaged in in the past with Alec added up, in reality, to no experience at all. Yet, though she was glad in a way that her first real taste of love should have been at the hands of an expert lover like Lorenzo, at the same time she was aware of a pang of regret.

It would be so easy to develop a taste for such loving, and she knew that this first time must also be her last.

He was easing himself upright and drawing her up with him. 'How about a swim before we go indoors?' He took her hand in his. 'Come and join me.'

Beth shook her head, feeling suddenly uncomfortable and acutely conscious of her naked state. The situation was ridiculous. None of this ought to have happened. And now all she wanted was to get out of it with as little fuss and delay as possible.

'I won't,' she told him. 'I think I'll get dressed now. You go ahead and swim if you like.'

'Are you sure?' He looked vaguely disappointed. As she shook her head firmly, he shrugged resignedly. 'OK, then. I'll just do a couple of lengths.'

Beth watched as he dived cleanly into the water, making barely a ripple as he headed for the far side. Then, with unseemly haste, she grabbed her discarded clothing—her underwear and blue denim sun-dress—and rapidly set about making herself decent again. All at once she felt awkward and hot with embarrassment, and desperate for this crazy interlude to end.

She had scarcely finished dressing when he popped up again beside her, pulling himself easily from the water to stand dripping before her in dark naked splendour. 'Dressed already?' He regarded her quizzically as he grabbed a towel to quickly rub his hair before tying the towel loosely around his waist. 'You could have borrowed a robe,' he told her. 'There are plenty in the changing-rooms.'

'I know, but I think I ought to be leaving now.' She glanced at her watch. 'It's getting rather late.'

Lorenzo raised his eyebrows. 'Leaving? Don't be silly. You're not going anywhere, *cara mia* Beth.'

He had slid an arm round her waist as he'd said it, and suddenly the touch of him felt awkward and strange. Beth felt herself stiffen.

'No, really. I must leave now. I don't know about you, but it's time I was in bed.'

Responding to her strangeness, he had dropped his arm away, but now he was gently taking hold of her shoulders, and swivelling her round to look into her eyes. 'I had rather hoped we might be going to bed together. I would like very much to spend the night with you.'

The very notion, for some reason, sent a dart of cold panic piercing through her. Didn't he realise that this encounter should never have happened? Couldn't he at least have the grace just to let her go now? 'That's out of the question.' She stepped aside brusquely. 'I'm sorry, but you appear to have got quite the wrong idea.'

The dark brows drew together. 'Quite the wrong idea?' He dropped his hands away, but seemed to hold her with his eyes. 'The idea I'd got was that you and I had become lovers. Are you trying to tell me I'm mistaken about that?'

Beth felt like weeping. What had she got into? She might have known that with Lorenzo nothing would be simple.

She stared down at the tiles. 'We have not become lovers. What happened was simply an aberration. I want to make it perfectly clear that it is never going to happen again.'

'I see. You surprise me.' The black eyes had hardened. 'But you are right; it is as well to make things perfectly clear.' He turned away from her impatiently, then paused to inform her in curt, hostile tones, 'However, that changes nothing as regards your remaining here. It's far too late for you to drive back alone—and, I can assure you, I have no intention of getting dressed just for the privilege of accompanying you.' His eyes bored into her, daring her to challenge him. 'You shall remain here for the night—and don't worry, I won't bother you. You can have one of the spare rooms. There are plenty to choose from.'

Amid her confusion Beth was growing angry. She was damned if she would be dictated to like this! 'I'd rather just go home, and I don't mind going alone. There's absolutely no need for you to go to the trouble of accompanying me!'

He glowered down at her, his wide lips thinning. His jaw had tightened. His cheeks were stiff with anger. 'You're suggesting that I allow you to return alone in the dark to an empty house? I'm sorry, but I will not hear of it!' he informed her. Imperiously he turned away again. 'You're spending the night here. That is all there is to it! We shall discuss it no further!'

In the end the argument had seemed scarcely worth pursuing. As much as she hated to bend to his will, this pointless bickering was giving Beth a headache. She felt suddenly as tense as the strings of a violin.

In angry silence she followed Lorenzo indoors, refusing even to glance at him as he showed her to her room.

'I hope you'll be comfortable,' he said, his tone formal. Then, without waiting for her answer, he stepped out into the corridor and closed the door with a sharp click behind him.

That she would be comfortable, at least physically, was beyond discussion. The room was luxurious to the point of sheer opulence, with a huge double bed spread with silk covers in the same rich dark blue as the draperies. There was a sofa, a writing-desk, an assortment of chairs, and a selection of paintings arranged on the walls that many a gallery would have been proud of.

Beth kicked off her shoes, pulled back the silken cover and dropped down tiredly on to the bed. Normally she would have found pleasure in such surroundings, but somehow the extravagant beauty of the room only seemed to increase her inner tension.

She had no business being here. She did not belong. And, what was more, she did not want to. And it had been utterly wrong and unfair of Lorenzo to insist on keeping her here for the night as though she were his prisoner.

She closed her eyes and sighed. He had done it out of malice, because she had turned down his offer to share his bed tonight. And it was just another example of his overbearing nature. In every situation he just had to be in control.

She laughed to herself bitterly and turned her face to the pillows. She despised him, she hated him, she could not bear the sight of him—and yet, less than an hour ago, she had allowed him to make love to her.

No, not simply *allowed*, she corrected herself
miserably. She had *wanted* him to make love to
her. She had virtually invited him.

She sighed and waited for the appropriate sense
of horror to grip her heart and fill her with
remorse. But she felt no horror, and no remorse
either, and that was really the strangest part of
all.

For it was as though what had happened had
been ordained to happen by some power greater
than either him or herself. She could not regret
it, because she could never have prevented it. She
felt that strongly—however illogical it was.

At the same time she was equally strongly
certain that she must never allow it to happen
again. It had been something that had happened
in isolation, an intimacy divorced from the two
people they really were. Above all, it had most
definitely not, as Lorenzo had seemed to take for
granted, been the start of some sort of love-affair
between them.

Heaven forbid! She shuddered at the thought.
He was the last man in the world she would have
a love-affair with!

Acknowledging that somehow made her feel
better. All at once her headache disappeared.
Feeling less like a prisoner and more in control
of her own destiny, she slid from the bed and
slipped off her sun-dress, then dropped it with
her underwear on to a chair. He was holding her
here at the villa temporarily, just as he had

temporarily possessed her body, but neither act had any real significance.

She padded across the carpet and climbed into bed, feeling the soft silk sheets cool against her skin. By tomorrow, with any luck, his male pride would have mended and he would have recovered from his anger at her rejection of him. Perhaps also, she prayed, he would have the good taste never to refer to this evening again.

The bedside lamps snapped off at the touch of a switch and Beth sank back gratefully against the pillows. Perhaps, she thought with sudden optimism, now that she had made that gesture of co-operation regarding her suspicions concerning Mariella's whereabouts he might also agree to drop his vendetta against Giles and allow her stepbrother to come out of hiding.

She closed her eyes and let sleep wash over her. All things considered, it had been quite a day!

'So, what's your verdict? Are they to your taste?' Lorenzo's tone was bantering as he came to stand behind her.

Beth did not turn round. She remained with her back to him, slightly resenting his intrusion. 'I like them very much,' she answered truthfully. 'They're Carillos, if I'm not mistaken?'

'Indeed they are.' He sounded surprised at her knowledge. 'Are you familiar with the work of Carillo?'

'Only via catalogues and magazines. We don't come across many paintings of such calibre in our little framing business, I'm afraid.' She turned then to look at him. 'They must be worth a fortune.'

They were standing in the hallway of the Villa dei Cesari where the collection of paintings was tastefully displayed. The paintings had caught Beth's eye on her way to the breakfast-room and she had paused with excitement to admire them. Luigi Carillo was one of her favourite modern painters.

But, suddenly, her mind had emptied of what they were talking about, for the moment her eyes had alighted on Lorenzo's face the strangest sensation had gone shooting through her. For an instant she was back by the pool last night and the man who stood before her was making love to her.

Her insides curled deliciously. Her heart almost stopped beating. And suddenly she could scarcely bear to be so near him without reaching out a hand to touch him.

He was dressed in a pair of light blue trousers and a dark blue short-sleeved open-necked shirt. And in the lightness of the hall, all pale marble and high windows, he was a dark and vivid, overpowering presence—and far more extraordinarily good to look at than any of his collection of Carillos!

What feeble, romantic drivel! Beth instantly chastised herself, dimly aware that he was saying, 'Yes, I believe they're quite valuable.' She pulled herself together as he went on to inform her, 'I bought them a number of years ago.'

'You made a good investment.' Beth was striving to sound normal, though her heart was still beating most erratically. 'In the past couple of years, from what I've heard, his paintings have increased ten times in value.'

Lorenzo smiled, she thought, a trifle condescendingly. 'I did not buy them as an investment. I bought them simply because they pleased me. I have no intention of cashing in on their increased value. They will remain here on my walls, exactly where they are now.'

One thing was for certain, this morning-after encounter had failed to affect him as it was affecting her. From the way he was looking at her, the way he was talking to her, one would never have guessed that less than twelve hours ago they had been making love beneath the moon.

Good, she decided, yet with a faint trace of resentment: he might have had the decency to betray *some* small emotion! It's probably because I refused to spend the night with him, she decided, glancing up to meet the shuttered dark gaze. And, for some reason, that explanation made her feel better.

'I never buy art as an investment.' With a small gesture he invited her to accompany him to the breakfast-room. 'And I make a point of refraining from purchasing what is fashionable.

It is my undeviating policy to buy only what appeals to me.'

Of course. It would be. She should have known that. In art, as in all things, he would go his own way. Hadn't she decided, right from the beginning, that he was born only to lead, never to follow?

'So, you too are a fan of Carillo?' he asked her, as they left the hallway and headed down a wide corridor. 'It is nice to know that we share the same tastes. At least...' he paused and looked straight at her '...we would have something to talk about in bed...were such a situation ever to arise again.' Unrepentantly, he met the angry flash of her eyes. 'Conversation after love-making can sometimes be so difficult.'

Beth was totally taken aback and faintly shocked by the tasteless tenor of his humour. She caught her breath and assured him quickly, 'Well, it's not a difficulty you need fear encountering with me!'

'Quite so.' He stood aside to allow her to pass before him as, at last, they reached the door of the breakfast-room. 'You and I need never fear such difficulties. As I said, we have so much in common.'

She was halfway through the door as he dropped in that last remark, and the only thing that stopped her from swivelling round to nail him with a suitably withering look was the sudden sight of the unexpected vision that awaited her in the breakfast-room.

Beth's jaw dropped open. She stopped in her tracks. 'Mariella! What are you doing here?' she gasped.

The girl grinned up at her from her brioche and coffee, and there was a twinkle in her eyes that eloquently suggested that she might very well ask Beth the same question! But she simply shrugged. 'I'm having breakfast. Do come and join me. Both of you!'

'But I thought...' Beth frowned in total bewilderment. Then she turned round accusingly to Lorenzo, but before she could say more, he had cut in.

'I forgot to mention that Mariella had returned.' He even had the gall to smile as he said it. 'She got back last night just after seven—a couple of hours before you turned up.'

'I was staying at a friend's,' Mariella chipped in now, as Beth and Lorenzo took their places at the table. 'I'd forgotten to tell Lorenzo I was staying overnight.' She pulled a face. 'I didn't half get a yelling!'

Lorenzo was watching his sister with dark eyes as he helped himself and Beth to coffee. 'Count yourself lucky that's all you got, *cara*. If you try pulling a stunt like that again, I promise I'll lock you in your room till the end of the summer.'

There was a flash of defiance across the table. 'No, you won't!'

'Try and stop me!'

'You have no right to make a threat like that! You seem to forget I'm not a child!'

'Then stop acting like one, *cara mia*. As soon as you start acting like an adult, I'll start treating you like one.'

There was a biting silence as Mariella flung down her napkin, and Beth could see that there were tears in her eyes. She glared at her brother. 'I hate you!' she exploded. 'I wish I'd never come to spend the summer with you!'

'You can go back to Rome whenever you please.' Lorenzo did not even bother to look at her as he helped himself to a croissant and butter. 'Mother, I'm sure, will be delighted to see you. And I,' he assured her, flashing a harsh look at her, 'won't shed any tears to see you go. I've already had enough of the disgraceful spectacle of my sister running after that English nobody like a bitch in heat.'

'Bastardo!' Mariella was leaping to her feet, almost toppling her chair over in her anxiety to escape. Then, gasping back the sobs that shook her, she was heading for the door.

In other circumstances Beth would have gone after her, for her heart went out to her; she longed to comfort her. But the situation between herself and the dei Cesari family was fast growing so complex and so muddled that she sensed it would be wiser to leave well alone.

Still, she threw Lorenzo a critical look. 'Don't you think you were a little hard on her just then?'

Lorenzo's eyes swivelled round to meet hers. 'No, I do not, as a matter of fact.' Then he turned away again. 'Please help yourself to croissants.'

So, she was being told that it was none of her damned business! That was to be expected, but all the same she insisted. 'She's only seventeen, you know. Girls are very sensitive at that age.'

'And rebellious, too. Yes, I am well aware of that. If I were to give her her head, she might well end up ruining herself, just to spite me and her mother.' He smiled a wry smile. 'Among her current rebellions is her refusal to continue next year with her studies. I'm sure you will agree that that would be most inadvisable? One can never overestimate the value of a good education.'

As he turned to meet her eyes again, Beth nodded in response. So in some areas, at least, he ran with the pack. His views on education were solidly conventional.

'I totally agree,' she answered, approving his stance. 'And I'm sure Mariella will realise that herself, once she's got over this rebellious phase of hers. She strikes me as being a very bright girl.'

'She's extremely bright.' He spoke the words with pride. 'And I intend to make damned sure she doesn't waste herself.'

Clearly he loved his sister very much. Touched, Beth felt her heart squeeze a little. Then she looked up at him, frowning. 'Why didn't you tell me, when I came here last night, that Mariella had already returned?'

'You didn't ask.' He drank back his coffee. 'Had you asked, I would have told you.'

The man was infuriating. Beth felt her blood boil. 'But you knew I was worried about her. Why didn't you just tell me?'

'You were worried about her?' He watched her over his coffee cup. 'Why should you be worried about my sister?'

'Because I'm that sort of person. I worry about people. Why else do you think I bothered to come here?'

He shrugged elaborately and laid his cup down. 'If that's your story, who am I to dispute it? But I have to confess I found it a little strange the way you came searching me out round the back of the house, while I was having a private swim in the pool. Most of my visitors arrive through the front door.'

Beth felt her cheeks flush at the baldness of the suggestion. Did he really believe she had come to see him on some sort of sexual assignation? 'I tried the front door,' she protested. 'I rang the bell several times. But no one answered, so I came round the back. I had no idea you were in the pool.'

'As I said before, who am I to dispute it?' A pair of sceptical black eyes raked her face. 'Not that I'm complaining. As it turned out, your visit proved to be really most agreeable. But if it was intended as a trade-off on your stepbrother's behalf, I'm afraid, *cara mia*, you were wasting your time.'

This time it was Beth who almost threw down her napkin and went stalking in protest out of the room. Quivering with anger, she swung round to face him, but already he was rising to his feet.

'Take your time over breakfast. There's no hurry. But I'm afraid I have to leave you now.' He glanced at his watch. 'Pressing business. I trust you'll find your own way back to the villa?'

Beth did not answer him. She was far too angry. Her insides were bubbling like a cauldron. And, suddenly, she could not wait another minute to be gone from him and from the Villa dei Cesari.

She sat still until he had left the room, and she heard a door along the corridor open and then shut again. Then she rose to her feet, shaking with anger, and on contemptuous, swift strides, made her exit.

May I drop down dead, she vowed to herself, if I ever pass through the doors of this house again! Sooner the very gates of hell than the iniquitous gates of the Villa dei Cesari!

The village was busy with local housewives doing their early morning shopping, but Beth paid little heed as she drove swiftly past them. All she could think of was of putting as great a distance, as quickly as possible, between herself and Lorenzo.

As at last she arrived outside Giles's villa, she felt herself relax a little. Soon she would be safe in her private little sanctuary, out of reach of the execrable Lorenzo dei Cesari!

But five minutes later, as she stepped through the front door, her sigh of relief froze in her throat.

In an instant the world seemed to have shattered about her. Surely, she thought numbly, I must be living in a nightmare!

CHAPTER SEVEN

THE place had been reduced to a virtual shambles. Someone, quite evidently, had been here in her absence and, without mercy, taken the whole house apart.

In a state of mild shock, Beth stood in the hallway, surveying the scene of chaos through the open doors to the rooms.

The bedrooms, the sitting-room and the study—all had been subjected to the same rough treatment. Furniture was toppled over, drawers were hanging open and their contents were strewn carelessly over the floors. It was a scene of total chaos. The sight of it made her blood run cold.

She dropped her bag on a chair. Who could have done it? And, even more to the point, *why* had they done it? Something told her that the intruders had not been mere thieves.

In that very instant the phone began to ring. She spun round a little nervously and snatched up the receiver. 'Hello? Who is it?' she demanded, suddenly grateful to have someone to speak to.

To her infinite pleasure it was Giles's voice that answered. She recognised it instantly through the crackles. 'Beth, I heard through the grapevine that you're staying at the villa. I'm just calling to check that everything's OK.'

Beth sank on to the chair where she had dropped her bag. 'Well, I hate to tell you this, but it isn't,' she told him. 'We've been broken into and there's a terrible mess.'

'What did you say?' There was a horrified silence. Then, when she repeated her statement, Giles told her, 'Listen to me, Beth; don't do a thing. Don't call the police. Don't talk to anyone.' He paused as the crackles on the line became more insistent, then ended hurriedly, 'Just stay put and take care of yourself. I'm on my way back. I'll see you soon.'

After she'd laid down the phone Beth made a tour of inspection, tidying up as she went along. And it quickly became clear that the damage was minimal—a lightly chipped picture-frame and a spilt vase of flowers—and, from what she could make out, nothing had been taken.

That was a relief, but it also made her uneasy. It seemed to indicate that the intruders had been professionals and that they had been searching for something in particular—not just for videos or music systems to steal.

What worried her, too, was Giles's insistence that she refrain from involving the police. Did that mean he knew who the intruders had been? Did he plan on dealing with them personally?

And suddenly she was aware that an uneasy suspicion was taking shape inside her own head. Perhaps she, too, knew the identity of the intruders—or at least the identity of the person who had sent them. And she felt sick with betrayal at the notion.

Could it possibly have been Lorenzo?

The more she thought about it the more likely it seemed. Hadn't he suggested to her once that, here in the villa, there must be some clue as to where Giles was hiding? He must have organised the break-in when he'd slipped off to order dinner.

As he had insinuated at breakfast, he had interpreted her visit as simply another shot at a sexual trade-off. And cynically he had co-operated, seducing her shamelessly, making love to her as though it were a game—all the while knowing that Giles's villa was being searched.

And, of course, it was the perfect explanation as to why he had been so adamant about her spending the night at his villa.

Beth had known that, for Lorenzo, making love to her had been an act of no real significance. But she had flattered herself that it had been an act of honest passion, that the madness that had possessed her had also possessed him. To realise now that it had all been calculated, from the first cynical kiss to the last empty caress, pained her as though he had shot an arrow through her.

She blinked back tears of humiliation. How he must have laughed to himself as he had made love to her! How he must be laughing still!

But at least there was one good thing to look forward to. Giles was on his way back. Soon everything would be cleared up. And, not a moment too soon, she could fly back to England and know that she would never see Lorenzo again.

'I'd no idea what he was up to. I knew he didn't like me, but I didn't know he was this crazy! Beth, I'm really sorry you had to get mixed up in this.'

They were seated in the sitting-room, drinking coffee after dinner—Beth and the extremely welcome Giles.

Beth smiled at him with sympathy, noting the drawn lines of his face. 'He's really got it in for you, I'm afraid. Though I'm glad to hear that it was only work, and not some threat of Lorenzo's, that caused you to disappear off the face of the earth.'

Giles laughed at that. 'I hadn't disappeared. I was only in France doing a bit of business. I'd no idea that you or anyone else was looking for me.'

'Well, I'm glad I've found you.' Beth poured them both more coffee and smiled across at him with a real sense of gratitude. Earlier she had explained the situation back home and he had at once insisted on phoning his father to reassure him that he would be over soon to sign the vital papers. 'I just find it strange,' Beth added, frowning, 'that you never received those letters from my mother.'

'That's not so strange,' Giles was quick to assure her. 'The post here isn't always terribly reliable. Sometimes letters take months to arrive.'

So, the only problem that remained now was Lorenzo.

'He's really mad at you over this business with Mariella,' Beth confided to him a little worriedly. 'And poor Mariella is very upset. Since you went away, she's been quite broken-hearted.'

Giles made a face. 'Silly little brat. I told her all along it was nothing serious.' Then, as he met Beth's look of disapproval, he added contritely, 'I never meant to hurt her.'

Beth smiled at him with sudden sympathy. Who was she to judge him, after all, when she too had been responsible for hurting someone? Still, remembering the promise she had made Mariella, she felt moved to advise him,

'I think you ought to talk to her. Have it out with her, face to face. Right now, she's feeling that you've just turned your back on her.'

Giles sighed. 'OK, then. But not right at the moment. Right now I want nothing to do with any of the dei Cesaris, not until I've had a couple of days' rest.' He shrugged wearily. 'As I'm sure you've gathered, it would be an utter waste of time even to think of reporting him to the police. He's far too influential around here. No one would believe he was responsible for the break-in. All it would do is simply stir up more trouble.'

Beth nodded. 'Yes, I think you're probably right. And, besides,' she reminded him, 'you've got to go to England. Ronnie's really anxious to get that mix-up sorted out.'

'I said I'd go, didn't I?' His tone was laced with impatience, but instantly he was apologetic. 'I'm sorry, I'm tired. I'd just like to have a day or two at home before I even think of doing anything. And, as I told you, I can't leave immediately. I'm expecting a very important phone call.'

He reached out suddenly to touch her arm. 'I know you said you were anxious to leave, but stay for a while. Keep me company.' He threw her a wink. 'I'd really appreciate it.'

To be truthful, Beth had wanted to say no, but like a fool she allowed herself to be talked into staying. Just for a few days, she promised herself firmly, and I shall be scrupulously careful to steer clear of Lorenzo. The thought of bumping into him made her blood freeze.

But, alas, Beth hadn't reckoned on Mariella!

She was spending an hour on the beach a couple of days later—alone, for as usual Giles was back at the villa, waiting impatiently for his phone call—when, out of the blue, Mariella showed up.

'Where have you been? I've been looking all over for you. I want to invite you to the house for dinner.'

'Dinner? No, I don't think that's possible.' Beth had scrambled to find an excuse to refuse.

'For a start, I don't think your brother would care for that idea.'

Mariella made a face. 'Oh, don't worry about Lorenzo. He and I have made it up. He'd be delighted to see you. And I insist that you come. I won't stop pestering you until you agree.'

Beth had resisted some more, but then reluctantly capitulated. 'She wasn't joking about pestering me,' she confided to Giles as she prepared to leave for her dinner date that very same evening. 'That young lady's used to getting her own way. If I'd said no, she'd only have started hanging round the villa. And don't worry, I won't give away anything about your being here,' she assured him as he threw her an anxious look. 'They couldn't drag it out of me with red-hot tongs!'

Mariella had arranged for a car to pick her up, and it was just after eight when the long dark Mercedes deposited Beth at the Villa dei Cesari.

As she stepped out, carefully adjusting her dress—a cornflower blue off-the-shoulder creation—a figure appeared suddenly in the main doorway, coming slowly down the steps towards her. And, in spite of all the cold indifference she had been practising, her heart nearly stopped dead in her chest.

Lorenzo was dressed in an immaculate black linen suit, with a white shirt, and a dark-striped tie at his throat. And caught in the hall lights that shone through the open doorway, he looked tall and broad-shouldered and impossibly handsome. The most handsome man that she had ever seen.

'Buona sera. E benvenuta!' Good evening and welcome. With a smile he held out his hand to greet her. 'I'm so glad you could make it, after all.'

At once Beth felt her poise grow shaky. In the abstract it was possible to resist him, to pretend he was just another mortal man. In the flesh it was a very different story. For some reason he turned her insides to jelly.

She looked into his face with its eyes like black lasers, smiling now, but still deeply unsettling, and tried not to remember how the hand that gripped hers had felt against her naked flesh. Yet, to add to her confusion, her blood leapt within her as she answered in a controlled voice, 'It's a pleasure to be here.'

'Come. Let us go inside now.' Lorenzo turned and began to lead her up the steps. Then at the top, as he paused and gestured to her to enter, he caught her eye for a moment and observed, 'Never have I seen you looking more beautiful. The colour of your dress, if I may say so, is almost as striking as the colour of your eyes.'

Beth muttered, 'Thank you,' and only just managed not to trip over the step on her way into the hall. Where was all this gallantry suddenly coming from? He's up to something! she told herself.

He led her through the hall, past the collection of Carillos, then down a wide corridor to a huge double doorway. A moment later, almost forgetting his presence in the sudden sense of wonder that seized her, she was stepping into the most beautiful room she had ever seen.

It was very large, the size of several tennis courts, and it was decorated in every shade of an emperor's jewels.

Sapphire-blue curtains, swagged and tasselled, flanked a row of open french windows, while garnet and ruby-coloured Persian carpets adorned the opal-tinted marble floor. Emerald and topaz cushions were tossed on damask sofas, themselves the deep bright blue of lapis lazuli, and golden lamps with pearl silk shades lit up the room with the sparkle of diamonds.

Transfixed, Beth stood mutely and blinked about her. For the very first time in her experience Lorenzo dei Cesari had been upstaged!

But that, she soon discovered, was merely temporary. As he strode past her dazed figure, heading for the french windows, his tall dark manliness instantly dominated the room.

He paused to glance at her. 'Won't you join me on the terrace? I suggest we have a drink before dinner.'

'What about Mariella?' As she followed him, Beth was suddenly very conscious that the two of them were alone. And to be alone with Lorenzo was the last thing she wanted. Simply being in the same room as him made her uneasy.

'She'll be with us in a moment.' As she stepped out on to the terrace, he was standing over a well-stocked refrigerated bar. 'What will you have to drink?' he asked her. Then he smiled. 'Don't worry, you're safe enough with me.'

That wasn't the case the last time, Beth observed privately, wishing he didn't make her feel so jumpy. Then studiously ignoring his dubious assurance, she informed him simply, 'I'll have a gin and tonic.'

'One gin and tonic coming right up.' As he set about his task, he gestured beyond the terrace. 'Why not enjoy the view while you're waiting? We have one of the best views in the district from here. In fact,' he added, 'if I may be immodest, I consider it to be one of the most beautiful views in the world.'

Since when was modesty one of his hang-ups? Beth pondered wryly as she crossed the stone-flagged terrace. But, as she reached the stone balustrade and leaned against it, she had to admit that modesty would have been misplaced.

They were on what, from the front of the house, was the ground floor. But from the edge of the terrace the ground fell away sharply, tumbling dramatically to the sea. To the right were the gardens, to the left a jagged cliff-face, and before them, seeming to stretch endlessly and forever, the still blue waters of the Mediterranean Sea.

A cluster of stars twinkled over the horizon while two crescent moons, one high in the heavens, the other its floating seabound image, lit up the night with a pale silver shimmer.

'It's quite magnificent,' she conceded over her shoulder. Then, envying him a little, she added quietly, 'You're very lucky to live in such a place.'

'Yes, I know it.' He came to stand behind her. 'We dei Cesaris are indeed exceedingly fortunate to have lived in such a place for so many generations. I hope one day when I have children that they'll appreciate it as much as I do.'

Beth had been about to turn round, but for an instant she could not, as a shaft of regret went knifing through her. It was his mention of the word 'children' that had undoubtedly done it, although her reaction really made no sense at all.

Since that night he had made love to her, it had never even occurred to her to worry that he might have made her pregnant. For some reason she had been feeling perfectly serene. Then this morning, on discovering that her period had started, she had experienced an illogical sense of disappointment—almost as though, somewhere in her subconscious, she had been hoping all along that she might be carrying his child.

I must be crazy, she told herself sharply as she gathered herself together and turned round to face him. Why on earth would I want to bear the child of a man whom I detest with all my strength?

He was standing very close, holding out her drink to her. There was a soft clink of ice cubes as it changed hands. And a dart as shocking as an electric current went shooting through her as their fingers briefly touched.

Beth looked up into his face, struggling out of her reverie, and forced herself to concentrate on what he was saying, as he continued, 'I would be quite happy to stay here all the time. Sometimes I wish I didn't have to go up to Rome so often.'

Beth had wondered about the frequency of his trips to the capital. 'And why do you have to go there so often?' she queried. 'Is because you have to visit your mother?'

Lorenzo laughed. 'Good heavens, no! My mother and I are close, but she has her own life.' He took a mouthful of his drink. 'My business is based in Rome. I have to go up to keep an eye on things.'

'What kind of business?' Beth was suddenly curious. Somehow she had assumed that he had no business, that he simply existed on the wealth of generations.

He seemed to read her mind. His eyes twinkled amusedly. 'I'm an architect, *cara* Beth, with a large practice in Rome and a couple of smaller offices, one in Milano and one in Paris.'

Beth was faintly impressed, though not at all surprised. Rather, his revelation was something she had half guessed at. Muretto was a small place with limited horizons. She had privately found it a little hard to accept that it could totally contain a man like Lorenzo dei Cesari.

'Your turn now. Tell me about yourself.' Lorenzo leaned casually against the stone balustrade and took another mouthful of his drink. The flicker of a smile touched the depths of his eyes. 'We are, after all, virtually strangers.'

Virtually strangers! Beth almost laughed in response. And yet, in spite of the physical intimacy they had shared briefly, she could not deny that he was right. They knew virtually nothing about one another. In sudden embarrassment she dropped her gaze.

'Tell me about your business, your family, the life you lead.' He continued to watch her. 'Really. I'm interested.'

Of course she didn't believe him. He was just being polite. His interest was no more than pre-dinner small talk.

Beth shrugged a little awkwardly. 'There's not much to tell. I come from a very ordinary family. My father was a salesman—he died when I was eight—and until I left home it was just my mother and me. I've always been interested in art and I've always wanted to run my own business. So, though I was advised against it——' she smiled suddenly '—as soon as I'd finished art college, that's what I did.'

'That doesn't surprise me.' Lorenzo smiled back at her. 'One thing that has always impressed me about you is that you have a mind of your own.'

'You mean I'm stubborn?' she reminded him with a twinkle.

'Stubborn as a mule.' His mouth quirked with humour. 'And this business of yours, this picture-framing business, is it doing well?' he asked her.

'Pretty well. I think we've finally turned the corner. But the first three years were pretty tough.'

'The first three years of any business are tough. Believe me, I remember, when I first started it was like emptying money down a bottomless pit. I was backwards and forwards so many times, trying to squeeze loans out of my bank manager, that I reckon I must have worn out his carpet.' He flashed her a sympathetic smile. 'I hope your bank manager's as understanding as mine was.'

As she glanced away hurriedly, his smile flickered and died. 'Ah, of course, I'd forgotten. You got the money from Alec.'

The chill of his disapproval seemed to cool the air between them. Beth could sense him mentally ending the sentence, '...and then, when you had no further use for him, you dumped him.'

But it hadn't been like that. 'I know you think I used him, but I swear to you I didn't. Alec wanted me to have the money—and I would never have let him lend it to me if I hadn't known that he could afford it.'

He turned once more to look at her, frowning a little. He doesn't believe me, she thought despondently. He's about to start tearing me to pieces again.

But, instead, he surprised her. 'Did you say "lend"? This fiancé of yours...you mean he only *loaned* you the money?'

'Of course he only loaned it! What did you think? Did you think he made me a present of it or something?'

The black eyes narrowed. 'As a matter of fact, yes. Considering he intended marrying you, that's exactly what I thought.'

Beth blinked at him. How wrong could he be? 'Oh, no. It was very much a loan. We drew up a formal, binding agreement, in which he gave me three years to pay it back, with interest to be calculated according to the bank rate.'

'Interest to be calculated according to the bank rate?' Lorenzo was staring at her, his eyes filled with astonishment, as though she'd suddenly grown two heads. 'I cannot believe this. This man you were to marry charged you interest on a loan?'

Beth was beginning to feel completely disoriented. This conversation had taken a most unexpected turn. She felt moved to enlighten him, 'Although he has a bit of money, Alec's not rich. He hasn't exactly got thousands to throw around.'

Lorenzo's astonishment, to her surprise, just grew sharper. 'And you would defend him?' he demanded, frowning at her. 'Didn't the arrangement strike you as peculiar?'

Beth shook her head. 'No, it didn't. I wasn't expecting any favours—I mean apart from the huge favour of him lending me the money in the first place.'

'But you could have got it from the bank on the very same terms! He wasn't doing you any favours!'

'The bank might have refused. That's what Alec said. He said they would probably consider me a poor risk.'

'Did you try a bank?'

'No, I took his word for it.' She shrugged apologetically. 'I used to be clueless over money matters.'

'You're not kidding!' Lorenzo leaned towards her and reached out to give her hair an almost affectionate ruffle. Then his expression hardened. 'I don't know what this ex-fiancé of yours was up to, but I would say you were very wise not to have married him.'

Beth blinked and smiled across at him, feeling a strange thrill of delight at this unexpected vote of confidence—and an even more delightful dart of pleasure, from her scalp to her toenails, at the way he had touched her.

He shook his head. 'And this loan of Alec's… Have you managed to pay it back yet?'

Beth nodded. 'Yes, it's all paid back. It was a struggle, but I did it.'

'You're quite a girl.' He let his eyes travel over her, his expression full of admiration. 'I reckon your mother must be very proud of you.'

Beth nodded, then hurriedly glanced away, hating the way the colour had flared to her face at this uncharacteristic barrage of compliments.

Why did she have to disintegrate so pathetically just because he had spoken a few kind words?

Thankfully at that moment Mariella appeared, looking breathtakingly lovely in a flame silk dress only a couple of shades darker than the red in Beth's cheeks.

'Sorry I kept you waiting,' she apologised. She kissed her brother affectionately, then she grinned at Beth. 'I just love that dress on you! That blue is perfect.' Then she took each of them by the hand and led them indoors. 'Shall we eat now? I'm absolutely ravenous!'

Dinner was served in the magnificent dining-room whose tall french windows opened out on to the gardens. And, far from being the ordeal that Beth had expected, it was a happy, thoroughly enjoyable evening.

As Mariella had assured her, she and Lorenzo were once again the best of friends, as though they had never been anything else. The affection between them, clearly stronger than their differences, shone from their faces for all the world to see. And the young girl was in good spirits, in spite of her secret heartache that was betrayed only rarely by a flash of sadness in her eyes.

But the star of the evening was undoubtedly Lorenzo. It was he who gave the conversation its special sparkle with his endless fund of anecdotes and funny stories. And, as he regaled his two delighted companions with tales of his friends and colleagues in Rome, Beth couldn't help

feeling very strongly that most of his perform-
ance was directed at her.

In a couple of hours, between the *prosciutto e
melone* and the peaches in wine with homemade
ice-cream, she had learned a great deal more
about him than she knew about some people she
had known all her life.

She was offered, for example, some insights
into his family. 'The reason there's such a huge
gap between me and Mariella is that it took my
parents eighteen years to get over the shock of
having me. Never again! they promised themselves. One tearaway in the family's more than
enough!'

'You, a tearaway?' Beth frowned mock-
disbelievingly, and Mariella burst out laughing.

'He was the absolute worst! He drove our
parents crazy! You should hear some of the
stories our mother tells about him!' She grinned
mischievously across at her brother. 'And now
it's my turn to give *him* a hard time!'

There were insights, too, into his spectacular
career as an architect. Like Beth herself, he had
built his business up from nothing, but he had
gone much further than she was ever likely to go.

'He would never admit it to you himself, but
he's considered to be one of the most brilliant
architects in Europe.' Mariella smiled proudly.
Then she added, teasing him, 'It's just as well
he's good at something!'

By the time the evening was, sadly, over, that
claim he had made earlier that they were 'virtually

strangers' Beth felt very strongly was no longer true.

He had revealed so much of himself—his tastes and his opinions—while cleverly coaxing her to reveal herself, too, that she felt now, in a strange way, that they knew each other well. And that that earlier flip comment of his that they had so much in common, much to her amazement, contained a great deal of truth.

Lorenzo had instructed a servant to have the car brought round for her. As the three of them sat on the front terrace, waiting for it to arrive, Beth stole a glance at him from beneath her lashes. He had been so charming to her this evening, and such delightful company, that it had felt at times as though he was out to captivate her heart.

Beth smiled to herself. He had the process backwards! First he had seduced her, and now he was seeking to win her over. In matters romantic, as in all things, the rules he played by were strictly his own!

Yet she was grateful to have had this evening with him. It made her feel better about having allowed him to make love to her. The Lorenzo she had seen revealed tonight she had thoroughly approved of. And more than that: she had found him deeply likeable. There were still vast areas of him that remained a mystery, but she no longer felt that the man she had made love with was a stranger. Even less did she feel him to be some kind of demon.

So why was he behaving so unreasonably with Giles? she quite suddenly found herself wondering. What she had discovered about him tonight didn't fit at all with that unpleasant side of him. He just didn't seem the type to conduct a petty vendetta.

There was the sudden sound of tyres crunching below them on the driveway. Lorenzo rose to his feet. 'That sounds like the car now.'

Together, the three of them took the stone steps down to where the car was waiting, then Mariella leaned to kiss her on the cheek. 'I'm so glad you came. It was a really super evening.'

Beth smiled back at her sincerely. 'I enjoyed it, too.' Then she was just about to offer her hand to Lorenzo, to thank him for his hospitality and wish him goodnight, when, to her absolute horror, he took her elbow and told her,

'You're not going home alone. I'm driving you, *cara*.' Then he was propelling her towards the waiting car.

But she could not allow it. It was far too risky with Giles in hiding at the villa. She made an effort to resist him. 'That's really not necessary...'

But already he had relieved the chauffeur of the keys and was opening the passenger door for her. 'Please don't argue,' he told her, ushering her inside then striding round to the driver's side to climb in beside her. 'As I told you once before, there's no way I would allow you to go home alone in the dark to an empty house.'

A moment later, he was driving out into the main street and heading swiftly for Giles's villa, a silent and deeply worried Beth seated reluctantly at his side.

CHAPTER EIGHT

BETH felt as though she were being driven to her own execution. Her limbs had turned to water, her mouth was as dry as sand and her heart was thumping so hard in her chest that she feared it might explode at any minute.

What if Giles, by some misfortune, should be waiting for her on the patio? Or watching out for her from some window? She had no idea what she expected might happen if Lorenzo and her stepbrother were to meet face to face, only that it was bound, at the very least, to be unpleasant. And she couldn't bear the thought of that.

The entire evening had been so special. Yes, *special*, she confirmed to herself without hesitation. She had secretly been looking forward, she now realised, to returning home and going off to bed to lie there and savour its specialness in private, and to try to sort out, once and for all, exactly what she felt for this man at her side.

She certainly didn't hate him, as she had in the beginning. She was even finding it difficult to maintain an attitude of disapproval. She sighed to herself, glancing across in his direction, feeling that increasingly familiar tightening in her throat that seemed to happen whenever she looked at him. The pure, simple truth of the matter was that negativity of any kind was starting to elude her.

He turned round to smile at her, eyes like black velvet. 'We must have dinner again some time soon,' he told her. 'Only, next time without Mariella.'

Her poor beating heart lurched crazily within her. She wasn't the only one who was changing. Lorenzo's entire demeanour towards her had altered, the abrasiveness and hostility of before quite vanished to be replaced by something approaching affection. And she could sense that the desire that shone from his eyes was as honest as the hunger that burned deep within her.

But, whereas half an hour ago this sudden change in him had delighted her beyond description, now, as they came in sight of Giles's villa, it was like a great weight on her heart. This unexpected and precious development between them simply meant that, suddenly, there was so much to lose.

As they reached the front gate, Beth turned to him nervously. 'You can drop me here. This is perfectly OK.'

But he ignored her entreaty and, with his next question, seemed to tap straight into her fear. 'I don't suppose you've had any word from Giles?'

The villa was in darkness, Beth was relieved to see, as he drew to a halt outside the front door. At least Giles was having the good sense not to announce his presence.

She cleared her throat. 'Have I heard from Giles? I'm afraid not. Not a word,' she assured him.

In the shadowy light of the street-lamps behind them, Beth was aware of his dark eyes on her as he switched off the engine and turned to face her. He seemed to look at her for a long time before he put to her, 'Come, *cara*, why are you holding out on me?'

Beth's heart leapt to her mouth. She could scarcely bear to look at him. 'I'm not holding out on you. I swear I haven't heard from him.'

There was another endless pause. Her heart almost stopped beating. Then a smile touched his lips. 'You misunderstand me. I was referring to a different question.' He raised one dark eyebrow. 'I invited you to dinner.'

Beth laughed nervously, relief flooding through her. 'Oh, that? Of course! I'd be delighted to have dinner with you.'

He was smiling at her. 'Excellent, *mia cara*. I shall give you a ring tomorrow to fix it.'

Then, with a smile and a warm look in his eyes, he was leaning towards her to embrace her, one hand in her hair, tilting her face towards him, as his lips came down to cover hers.

It was just as before, only even more irre-sistible, the thrill of excitement that went jolting right through her. As his mouth possessed hers, she felt the hunger within her well up into an un-stoppable tide. Breathlessly she pressed against the hand that caressed her, as with his tongue he

invaded her mouth's inner sweetness, sending a
shudder of white heat flashing through her,
lighting a throb of desire in her loins.

Her off-the-shoulder dress provided no
protection against the cool hard fingers that
sought her naked flesh. With a sigh he was
drawing her yielding body against him as with
one expert movement he slid the bodice lower to
allow him access to her breasts.

'Lorenzo, please stop!' It took all her strength
to say it, and she hated the sound of the words
as she spoke them. The last thing she wanted was
an end to this pleasure. But she knew only too
well where it was leading and she could not allow
him to make love to her now.

It had nothing to do with her foolish promise
to herself that she must never allow him to make
love to her again. That edict had applied to the
stranger he had once been to her, the stranger
that, as of this evening, he had happily ceased
to be.

But, though she longed for him with her body
that burned at the touch of him, and with her
soul that ached to share again that sense of
oneness, with bitter certainty she knew she must
refuse him. She simply had no choice in the
matter.

With the comforts of the villa there for the
taking, he would be unlikely to settle for the back
seat of the car. And, were she to insist on such
an arrangement—for he must on no account enter
the villa!—he was only bound to wonder why.

And why? was the question in his eyes now as he drew back a little and frowned down at her. 'What's the matter, Beth? Are you asking me not to make love to you?'

Beth wriggled away from him. 'Yes, that's what I'm asking.'

'Perché?' he demanded. 'Why? Is something the matter?'

'Nothing's the matter. I just don't want you to.'

He smiled at her wryly. 'I don't believe you. That's not what your body was telling me a moment ago.' He leaned towards her. 'Come, *mia cara*. Let's go indoors. We'll be more comfortable there.'

Damn him for insisting! Beth stiffened in sudden panic. 'I said no! Didn't you hear me? What's the matter, are you deaf? Or is it just too much for your male vanity to cope with when a girl has the nerve to reject your advances?'

She knew she was over-reacting. A simple 'no' would have sufficed. But suddenly she felt like a helpless kitten trapped in a corner by a pack of wild bloodhounds. It was pure unthinking animal instinct that made her spit and flash her claws.

And, as she looked into his eyes, grown dark and shuttered, she realised it was not Giles she was protecting, but herself. More terrible than anything he might do to Giles would be her despair if he was to discover that she had been lying to him.

She turned away abruptly and began fumbling for the door-handle. 'If you don't mind, I think I'll say goodnight now.'

He did not try to stop her, but, as she half staggered out on to the driveway, he had emerged from the driver's side and was standing before her. At the look of mute horror on her face, he held up one hand to reassure her. 'Don't worry; I'm not planning to drag you inside and rape you. I simply want to see you safely indoors before I leave you.' His tone had acquired an edge of hostility that, even through her anxiety, touched Beth's heart with ice. The evening had been ruined, all the rapport between them vanished. In a flicker he had been transformed into the enemy of before.

Struggling to sound normal, apologetic even, she assured him, 'There's really no need. I wish you wouldn't bother. I'll be perfectly fine now on my own.'

'But I insist.' His hand was on her elbow. 'I promise you, it's no bother at all.' Then he was guiding her stiff, resisting body across the flag-stones to the front door. He turned to smile at her grimly, his free hand extended. 'The key, please. I need it to open the door.'

Beth looked into his face, her soul sick with misery, and was tempted to beg him one last time to let her go into the house alone. But the more she begged, she knew for certain, the more he would insist on having his way.

Inwardly she sighed and reached into her bag. There was absolutely no point in trying to resist him. What happened now was in the hands of fate.

She handed him the key, not daring to look at him. Then, like a victim of the guillotine waiting for the blade to fall, she stood watching him with fear clutching at her heart as he turned the key and pushed the door open, then reached inside to switch on the light.

Nothing happened. Beth dared to breathe again, as he stood aside and bade her enter the hall. She forced a smile and turned to thank him, but before she could utter a single syllable her jaw dropped open in horrified dismay as he stepped into the hall behind her and closed the door.

'I'll just make a quick check of the rooms, if you don't mind.' He paused and held her eyes for a moment. 'I take it you have no objection?'

Beth's mouth had gone as dry as sawdust. 'I wish you wouldn't,' she protested weakly. 'I can assure you none of this is necessary.'

'How can you know? Someone could be hiding here.' Again he paused and regarded her closely. 'You must admit that is a possibility, is it not?'

Beth looked back at him miserably. 'If you insist on looking, look,' she told him weakly. Since she could not stop him from doing what he must do, at least let him have mercy and get it over with quickly.

She followed him through into the sitting-room, then, her legs suddenly trembling too violently to support her, she perched tremblingly on the edge of an armchair as he made a quick inspection of the kitchen, then disappeared off to do likewise with the bedrooms. It was just a matter of seconds now before he came face to face with Giles.

'All clear. You can relax now.' Suddenly he was standing in the doorway, watching her. 'You can sleep easy in your bed tonight. There's nobody here but you and me.'

'Nobody?' Beth stood up slowly. Was he joking or what?

'Nobody, *cara* Beth. Does that surprise you? Were you expecting there to be somebody hiding under your bed?'

'Of course I wasn't!' She laughed a little nervously, unsure whether she ought to feel relieved or concerned. Where was Giles? What on earth had happened to him? How could he have simply disappeared?

With a strange smile Lorenzo was crossing the room towards her, like a lion, she thought, stalking his prey. As he smiled, there was a mysterious glint in his eyes. 'I'll say goodnight now,' he purred, standing before her. 'No doubt you're anxious to get to bed.'

Beth swallowed drily. 'Yes, I am rather tired.' And that, at least, she reflected, was no lie. Suddenly she felt limp from nervous exhaustion, yet relieved and grateful at the same time. She'd been all the way to the foot of the guillotine and somehow, miraculously, she'd survived!

She felt a sudden surge of optimism. She had not been unmasked. And perhaps now she could undo some of the damage she had done.

She smiled at Lorenzo apologetically. 'I'm sorry for my rudeness earlier in the car. I really don't know what got into me.' As he reached out to touch her cheek with his fingers, she held her breath and suppressed a shiver. 'I hope you're not still angry with me?'

'Angry? Of course not.' He tilted her chin. 'Why on earth should I be angry?'

Then his free hand was sliding like a charm round her waist and, ever so gently, he was drawing her towards him. As his lips bent to touch hers, Beth felt her bones melt, and suddenly she was wishing that, after all, the evening might have ended rather differently. But, already, he was drawing away and bidding her goodnight. 'I mustn't keep you from your sleep.' He smiled and started to turn away, then paused as if suddenly remembering something. 'Oh yes, of course. I almost forgot to give you these.' As he spoke, he reached into his inside jacket pocket and withdrew a sheaf of colour photographs.

He held them up before her, as if with tongs, then with a contemptuous gesture tossed them down on the nearby table. 'In case you have nothing to read in bed tonight, you can amuse yourself by flicking through these.'

Beth's eyes had flown to the scattered photographs, and as she recognised them she felt sick to her stomach. For they were photographs of herself and Giles, taken over the past two days.

Suddenly she could not speak. Lorenzo had known all evening that she had been deceiving him.

As she paled, his eyes flayed her. 'You're quite an actress! Lies come tumbling from those pretty lips of yours like cherries dropping from a tree.' He regarded her now as though she were vermin. 'God help any man,' he ground out, 'who's fool enough ever to believe in you. You don't know the beginning of the meaning of trust. If you ask me, that fiancé of yours is well shot of you— which is exactly what I intend to be, too!'

Then, with a look that turned her bones to powder and pierced like a lance through her bleeding, aching heart, he turned on his heel and strode out of the room, through the hall and out of the front door, as though she had suddenly become so repugnant to him that he could no longer bear to breathe the same air.

Beth wanted to cry 'Stop!', to go running after him, to prostrate herself at his feet and implore him to be merciful.

But she could not move. Her very soul had become paralysed. And all she could do, as she heard the door slam, was cover her stiff, ashen face with her hands and sink with a torn sob to the floor.

It was far too late in the day for tears. Tears could do her no good at all now. And yet she could not stop them. She wept like a baby. She wept until she had no tears left.

What was she crying for? she lay in bed and agonised. For Lorenzo and the way he so openly despised her? For the loss of a love that had never been hers? For a dream that had ended before it had begun? Or was she simply weeping for the unfairness of it all?

For it *was* unfair, she thought forlornly, as she flicked through the photographs of herself and Giles. The pictures damned her as a liar, for they proved conclusively that Giles had been hiding here.

There were photos of them having lunch together in the kitchen, laughing over some joke together as she cooked dinner, chatting in the sitting-room over a bottle of wine. But the evidence itself was unfair and misleading.

OK, so she had lied! Giles had been here all the time. But why was she being made to feel that she had committed some crime?

She had been loyal to Giles because he was her stepbrother and because she could see no sense in Lorenzo's vendetta. That her loyalty had led her into conflict with him was something that she deeply regretted. But she'd had no choice but to act as she had. Surely, if he were reasonable, Lorenzo ought to see that?

Beth laughed to herself hollowly. Reasonable? Lorenzo? When had he ever been guilty of being reasonable? He was a man who saw things strictly from his own point of view. It was unlikely that he was even aware that there might be any other!

Her insides curled with misery as she remembered how he had looked at her and heard again the cruel words he had spoken. And too late she understood his strange behaviour—his queries regarding Giles and whether or not she had heard from him. He had been offering her one final chance to come clean. And she had just lied all the more and continued to insist that she had no idea where her stepbrother was.

But he understood nothing of the sentiments that had motivated her. He would not hate her so fiercely if he did.

In the end it was partly her resentment at his misunderstanding of her that goaded Beth into making her next move. For the more she dwelt on it the more her hurt turned to anger. She owed it to herself to set the record straight!

But the more immediate reason for her trip to the Villa dei Cesari two days later was to find out about Giles. For since that fateful evening he had not returned to the villa. And if anyone knew where he was that person was Lorenzo.

It was just after lunchtime as she drove through the village. The shops were closed for the afternoon siesta and there was scarcely anybody about.

Beth had chosen her time deliberately. It was a neutral time of day, a time of day when nobody had appointments, nor any particular business to see to. He would have no excuse for refusing to see her, for she doubted very much that it was his habit to sleep, and there could be no fear of his misinterpreting her reason for being there, as there might have been had she chosen to go in the evening.

After parking her car she marched boldly to the front door, took a deep breath and rang the doorbell. This time she would wait until someone answered. She would not make the mistake of surprising him in the pool!

She had rung twice and was on the point of ringing again when she heard footsteps approach on the other side of the door. A moment later the door swung open and her stomach lurched violently with pleasure and anguish as she found herself looking into a pair of black eyes.

It was Lorenzo and he was evidently less than delighted to see her. He scowled down at her darkly. 'What do you want?'

'I want to see you.' Her heart was beating wildly. She had not expected him to answer the door himself.

'So, now you've seen me.' He regarded her coldly. 'Now you can go back to where you came from.'

For a moment he seemed about to close the door in her face. Beth stepped forward quickly. 'I want to talk to you,' she cut in.

'Talk to me?' He raised one jet black eyebrow. 'What on earth would you want to talk to me about?'

'About Giles—among other things.' She looked straight at him. 'You'd better let me in. I won't go away.'

A flicker of irritation darkened his features. 'Is that supposed to be a threat?' He smiled at her mockingly. 'Believe me, *cara mia*, if I decide you are to leave, leave is precisely what you'll do!' He paused. 'However, it might be amusing to allow you in for half an hour. I wonder what lies you've come to tell me this time?' He stood still. 'Be my guest. After all, I wasn't doing anything else.'

Damn his arrogance and his condescension! As Beth followed him through the elegant hallway, with its collection of Carillos on the walls, that flash of pained pleasure she had felt on first seeing him was mellowing nicely into a glow of antipathy. She must not allow him to overawe her, nor her own confused and powerful feelings for him, even for a moment, to take control.

Disdain was the only emotion she must allow to possess her. She must feel for him the same cold contempt that he so clearly felt for her.

He led her through to the same sumptuous reception-room where he had entertained her once before. But this time Beth glanced neither to right nor to left as he bade her sit on one of the blue damask sofas.

'Would you care for a drink?' He was standing over a trolley, where a selection of bottles and glasses was laid out. 'I'm having a brandy. I find brandy most soothing. A perfect antidote to unpleasant company.'

'Then I ought to have a double.' Beth smiled humourlessly back at him. Let him mock all he wished. She couldn't care less.

He poured two drinks, then on long, hurried strides crossed the ruby carpet to hand her one. And as his fingers contemptuously brushed against hers, much to Beth's angry consternation a shaft of electricity shot down to her toes.

As she pulled herself together again, he sat on the sofa opposite her. '*Salute!* Cheers!' He raised his glass and drank. Then he leaned back against the jewel-bright cushions. 'So, to what exactly do I owe this displeasure?'

Beth was dressed all in white, he from head to toe in black, and as he laid one sun-browned arm along the arm of the sofa he seemed as relaxed and at ease with himself as she was awkward, stiff and tense. The blue eyes met the black with a flash of resentment. How dared he sit there like some Oriental pasha granting an audience to one of his poor slaves?

She glowered across at him. 'You owe this displeasure to the fact that I want you to tell me where Giles is. I haven't seen or heard from him since that night you took me back to the villa. I think you probably know where he is.'

He shrugged and drank. 'I can tell you where he is. I can even arrange for you to visit him, if you like.'

'I can arrange my own visits, thank you very much. It will be quite sufficient if you just tell me where he is.'

Lorenzo smiled. 'My pleasure, I assure you. Your dear stepbrother is precisely where he ought to be—languishing in a Roman gaol.'

By a whisker Beth managed to hold on to her glass. Her eyes boggled disbelievingly. 'You're having me on!'

'Not in the slightest, I'm happy to say. He was transferred to Rome from the local prison yesterday afternoon.'

He really was serious! It was not some sick joke. 'But what on earth is he supposed to have done?'

'You mean you really don't know, *cara mia*? Such innocence is very touching.' With a sceptical smile, he took a mouthful of his brandy, then laid the glass down on the table by his side. 'The charges that have been brought involve deception and dishonest dealing, a variety of other felonies and, of course, trafficking in drugs.'

'Trafficking in drugs? I don't believe you! Giles could never be involved in such a thing!'

'Oh, come off it, Beth! Do you take me for an idiot? You knew damned well what was going on.' Impatiently Lorenzo had jumped up from his seat, snatching his half-empty brandy glass from the table as he strode back to the bar table to fill it up again.

'For all I know, you were even actively involved.' He glanced up from what he was doing and blazed a look at her. 'Perhaps you were in for a cut on his latest drugs venture or his latest crooked business deal?'

'How can you say such a thing?' Beth was almost gagging. 'All of what you're saying is pure invention. You know the reason why I'm here!'

'Because of your stepfather? A good cover story. I congratulate you. I was almost taken in.'

Beth stared at him in horror. How could he say this? How could anyone believe such a hideous blasphemy? Suddenly her entire body was trembling. 'What you're saying is crazy!' she breathed.

'Crazy, is it? You mean you're really trying to tell me you had no inkling of what was going on? You didn't know that the reason Giles was skipping around Europe was to try and avoid all the people who were after him? His creditors, the people he'd swindled and the enemies he'd made among the drug-dealing fraternity. Believe me, Giles had plenty of enemies.'

Beth looked straight back at him, her stomach churning. 'I've already told you. I knew nothing at all.'

'I suppose you know nothing about the break-in, either?'

Beth shook her head.

'Then let me tell you. That break-in—about which you kept suspiciously quiet—was the work of some old pals of Giles, some pals he'd done out of a large chunk of money. They'd heard he had some stashed away at the villa and decided to come and help themselves.

'But Giles wasn't that careless. The money was with a friend—a certain Giacomo who frequents La Luna Verde. When Giles came back from France—because the French police were on to him, not because he was worried about you, incidentally—Giacomo was supposed to get the money to him here so that he could skip to South America. We've known for a long time he was planning to go there and that's why I was so anxious to track him down. I was afraid we might lose him for good.'

He smiled maliciously. 'But his plans came unstuck. Giacomo and the money have mysteriously disappeared.'

So, that was the phone call Giles had been waiting for! Beth frowned across at Lorenzo as something occurred to her. 'But he couldn't go to South America! He had to go to England first.'

Lorenzo drained his drink. 'Go to England? That's the last place he intended going. The British police have been after him for years. That's why he originally moved to Italy.'

It was like a horror story. Beth could still scarcely believe it. 'But where do you fit in?' she demanded curiously. 'Were you one of Giles's creditors or something?'

He had sat down on the arm of the sofa opposite her. 'Not me personally, but a friend of mine. Giles completely ruined him and he ended up by taking his own life.' He stared for a moment into his brandy glass and his voice cracked with emotion as he went on to elaborate, 'I swore I'd get the guy who cheated my friend, but I never dreamed he'd end up in my own back yard. Of course, Giles never knew that I knew all about him, nor that I'd passed on what I knew to the local police. He hadn't a clue that I was after him—although he must have begun to suspect when you told him I was looking for him.'

He paused and ran his long fingers roughly through his hair. 'But, quite frankly, I wasn't interested in some personal vendetta. He owes a lot more people than just that friend of mine. What I wanted was for him to pay his debt to society, in a prison cell, for a very long time.'

If all he was telling her was true—and Beth had no reason to disbelieve him, though it was hard to accept such things about her step-brother—then, she had to agree, that was the punishment Giles deserved. 'And to think I thought that all you had against him was his relationship with Mariella! I was beginning to think you were a bit obsessed with that.'

Lorenzo smiled wryly. 'I was a bit obsessed. I would more than happily have wrung his neck just for that transgression alone!' Then he sat back in his seat and sighed a little wearily. 'But these things happen. Mariella was unwise, but seduction is scarcely a hanging offence. And I'm sure she gave him plenty of encouragement. She was quite genuinely bowled over by him.'

He shook his head. 'Thank goodness it's all over.' Then he glanced across at Beth, his gaze strangely shuttered. 'I suppose now you'll be going back to England?'

Beth nodded. 'Eventually, but not just yet. Since it looks as though Giles won't be able to make it to England, I'll have to figure out a way of getting his signature on those documents of his father's——' She broke off suddenly and narrowed her eyes at Lorenzo. 'You *do* believe that's the reason I came here? You don't seriously think I was mixed up with Giles? Nothing could be further from the truth, I promise you.'

Lorenzo did not answer. He frowned suddenly. 'Why did you once tell me that without Giles's signature on those documents your mother ran the risk of ending up homeless?'

'It's a complicated story.' She was surprised that he remembered that hysterical little outburst in the piazza in Saranno. But, though it hardly seemed to matter now, she was loath to elaborate. He was bound to blame Giles for the whole legal mix-up and the thought that he might be right in doing so secretly appalled her.

He smiled at her evasion, but mistook her reasons. 'Loyal to the very end, I see.' Then he rose to his feet and, without looking at her, told her, 'In spite of that, no, I don't believe that you knew what he was up to. You can relax. You've convinced me.'

As she smiled a huge smile of relief he added, 'These papers that need signing... I'm sure you can arrange to have them signed here. I'll put you on to a good lawyer who can help you.' He crossed to a desk and returned with a printed business card. 'Give this guy a ring. Say I recommended you.'

Beth smiled at him gratefully. 'That's very good of you.' And she felt a warm glow spread through her that he was prepared to assist her.

Undoubtedly her task would be a great deal easier if she had Lorenzo at her side. And, what was even more important than that, if they could only spend a little time together, whatever misunderstandings still existed between them could surely finally be ironed out. It would be a kind of breathing space. Precisely what they needed. A chance to get to know each other even better and to discover what their real feelings were for one another.

He was standing in front of her, still looking down at her, his hands thrust into his trouser pockets. 'I hope you'll be successful. I'm sure you will be.' Then, as she smiled in gratitude, he added in a cool tone, shattering her heart into tiny pieces, 'Neither Mariella nor I will be here to bother you. Tomorrow I'm taking her on holiday to Sardinia. We'll both be gone for the remainder of the summer.'

CHAPTER NINE

So BETH was all alone now at Muretto, with plenty of time at her disposal to sort out the muddle in her head. Only the muddle had miraculously de-muddled itself without any real assistance from her.

What was there to think about? she asked herself wryly, as she lay on the beach beneath a huge empty sky. She was in love with Lorenzo; she had always been in love with him, from that very first moment when she'd risen from the sea and glimpsed him standing by the big red sun-umbrella.

All the other emotions had been mere subterfuge, a shield against something she could not understand. Her head had told her he was evil, the kind of man to be reviled and despised, and her heart, though it had known better, had tried to co-operate by erecting against him a fragile wall of hate.

She lay very still and breathed very slowly as tears came rushing to her eyes. She had already wept too many tears for her folly. Over the past few days she had rarely stopped crying.

Yet, what would she have done differently if she had faced her feelings sooner? That was the question now going round in her head. And the answer was simple: she would have done *every-thing* differently. Starting with that love-scene by the swimming-pool.

If I had known I was in love with him, I would never have let it happen, she told herself bitterly on a wave of fresh pain. For I knew he was a difficult, an impossible man to love, a man incapable of loving in return. I should never have risked my heart by allowing him to make love to me. That was the rashest mistake of all.

For that physical coming together had affected her deeply. She had always known it. She knew it more certainly now. As he had entered her body, he had entered her soul also, and now it was impossible for her to shake free of him. He was part of her, yet absent, and the lack of him was terrible. She felt empty; a chipped, discarded vessel.

She bit her lip as the agony tore through her, an agony that was destined to outlast eternity. For what tragedy could be greater than to feel so deeply for a man who had turned his face forever against love?

It was two days later that Beth received a long-distance phone call from her friend and business partner, Jacqui, in London.

'I've got news for you,' Jacqui told her. 'Not exactly what you might call good news, but definitely something to make you feel better about walking out on Alec.'

Beth frowned into the telephone. 'Alec?' she repeated. It seemed like a lifetime since she'd last thought of her ex-fiancé. 'What sort of news do you have about Alec?'

Jacqui seemed to hesitate for a moment. 'First, I want to know that you haven't changed your mind about him. I mean, you haven't suddenly decided you want to marry him after all?'

Beth laughed, the first time she'd laughed for ages. 'Good heavens, no! That's the last thing on my mind!' If only Jacqui knew about Lorenzo and all that had happened since they'd last met! But she'd no intention of going into that now, and anyway, suddenly, she was curious. She prodded Jacqui. 'So, come on, tell me. What's this news that you phoned to tell me?'

'Well...' Jacqui took a deep breath before continuing. 'It seems that your poor broken-hearted Alec has been playing something of a double game. He has a long-standing girlfriend out in Saudi. Jenny Wilkins met them on holiday together in Cyprus just a couple of days ago. It turns out this liaison has been going on for ages.' She paused on a note part triumphant, part apologetic, then hurried on to assure her friend, 'So, you see, you have nothing to feel guilty about regarding Alec. The man is nothing but a lying, cheating skunk.'

Beth found herself smiling. She thought she'd forgotten about Alec, but what Jacqui had just told her was good news indeed. For somewhere deep inside her there had been a smidgen of guilt remaining about the way she had broken off their engagement, and now it was completely washed away.

'Thank you, Jacqui. I'm glad you phoned to tell me. I just wish I'd known that a long time ago.'

'My pleasure, Beth. That's what friends are for.' Jacqui sounded relieved at her reaction. 'So, how are things going?' she enquired, changing the subject. 'Have you managed to track down your stepbrother?'

Beth pulled a face. If only Jacqui knew! 'Yes, I have,' she answered. 'It's quite a story. I'll tell you all about it when I get home. Trouble is I'm not sure when that'll be. I'm tied up with lawyers at the moment. But I'll be in touch. I'll let you know.'

'OK. Hey, Beth, I'd better go now; a couple of customers have just come in.'

Beth bade her farewell and hung up with a sigh. If only she could fly back to England right away and end the misery that staying here had become. For Muretto without Lorenzo was as desolate and empty as the proverbial far side of the moon— and so full of desperately painful memories that each day chipped away another corner of her heart.

She had been to see the lawyer that Lorenzo had recommended and he seemed confident that the papers could be signed in Rome.

'Leave it with me,' he'd told her. 'I'll contact your stepfather's solicitor in England and let you know the moment I hear anything.'

After that Beth phoned him daily, pushing him for news, and was delighted and amazed when, less than a week later, he informed her triumphantly, 'The papers are on their way over by special messenger, and I have an appointment with your stepbrother tomorrow afternoon.' He had paused for a moment. 'If you wish you can come with me, but your presence isn't strictly necessary.'

'In that case, I'll skip it.' Beth felt a little cowardly, but she had no desire to face Giles just yet. It had been hard enough explaining things to Ronnie and her mother when she had phoned home the other night.

Yet that phone call had also been unexpectedly joyful. 'Darling, you'll never guess,' her mother had told her, 'we've just received some marvellous news about Ronnie. There's been a remission. He's back on his feet again. I can't believe it! It's like a miracle!'

'It is a miracle! I'm so happy for you. But I think we should go ahead with these papers anyway. This legal mix-up needs to be sorted out.'

Fortunately, both her mother and Ronnie had agreed and had been happy to leave things in her hands—and Beth was overjoyed when the lawyer phoned her up the morning after his appointment in Rome and told her, 'Good news, *signorina*! The papers have been signed. Everything is now completely in order and you're free to go back home whenever you wish.'

Within the hour Beth had telephoned the airport in Rome and made an unconfirmed booking for the following evening.

'We'll get back to you tomorrow,' the booking-clerk promised. 'If you don't hear by lunchtime, give us a ring.'

So, after all, her mission here had been accomplished. Through her sadness Beth felt a small spark of triumph. Then, as a kind of celebration, after phoning her mother she decided to spend the afternoon in Muretto shopping for gifts to take back home.

She would buy nothing for herself, she resolved with Spartan firmness. She had no need of knick-knacks to remind her of Muretto. What she needed was something to help her forget.

It was a relaxing couple of hours, just pottering about the shops, and once she had finished buying her presents she stopped off for an orange juice and a pastry at one of the open-air cafés in the main piazza.

It was mid-afternoon and the streets were busy with local people, mostly, going about their business. Beth sipped her drink and gazed around her idly, enjoying all the mundane comings and goings, and reflected that it would feel strange to be back in England once again.

She enjoyed the Southern open-air way of life. It would feel odd to be shut up in the shop again.

She took a forkful of her pastry and cast the thought from her as tears threatened to prick at the backs of her eyes. It wouldn't feel odd. It would feel blessedly normal and, what was more, she couldn't wait to get back to England. In a couple of weeks from now, she told herself determinedly, Muretto would be no more than a hazy blur on her memory.

And then she saw him.

Her heart stopped dead. Lorenzo! He was here! He hadn't gone to Sardinia!

He had been striding through the crowd at the far side of the piazza, a tall dark figure in a light blue suit, and for a moment the whole world seemed to light up around him. But then, even as her heart began to beat again, far too quickly, like a steam hammer, he turned and disappeared through an open shop doorway.

Beth stared at the space where he had been as though she could will him to reappear before her. She wanted to jump up and go running after him. Her whole body suddenly throbbed with excitement and pain.

Fool! she chastised herself. You're seeing things again. It wasn't Lorenzo! It was just another hallucination!

For it wasn't the first time she had thought she had seen him, only to be proved wrong as she'd hurried towards some man and found herself facing a total stranger. This past week she seemed to have seen him on every street corner, at the wheel of every car, through every shop window.

And every time it happened her heart tore in two.

She turned away wretchedly. Thank heavens she was leaving. This endless torture was more than flesh and blood could suffer.

The next day, mercifully, was the day of her departure. Beth arose early, feeling weary, and showered quickly, then decided to have breakfast out on the patio.

After breakfast I'll start packing, she decided, then I'll spend the rest of the morning tidying up the villa and waiting for the airport to call.

She poured herself coffee and stirred in sugar. It was just a matter of hours now till she would be leaving this place forever. Surely she could manage to survive till then?

And then, to her horror, it happened again.

Just as she was about to take a mouthful of her coffee, he suddenly appeared at the bottom of the garden. He was walking up the path, heading towards her, dressed in cream trousers and a matching cream shirt.

Beth laid down her cup and blinked her eyes fiercely. What was the matter with her? Was she going mad? But when she looked again he was still there, only closer. And now suddenly she was hearing things as well as seeing them. She could have sworn she heard a deep voice bid her, *'Buongiorno.'*

He had come up the short flight of steps from the garden and was standing before her now on the patio. And at last she knew this was no hallucination. She could feel his warmth, smell the clean male scent of him. She could have reached out and touched him with her hand.

Lorenzo glanced down at her without smiling. 'I hope I'm not disturbing you. I was just passing. I thought I'd look in and see how you were.'

'Just passing?' Beth didn't know how to react to him. He seemed strange somehow, uncharacteristically reticent, and she, for her part, was suddenly quite incapable of thinking straight. 'What do you mean you were just passing? I thought you'd gone to Sardinia on holiday.'

'I had, but I'm back.' He motioned to the chair beside her. 'Do you mind if I sit down?'

Beth shook her head, registering dully that it was not at all like Lorenzo to require permission to seat himself. But the thought that filled her mind and caused her heart to race erratically was that he was actually here with her when she had expected never to see him again.

She said, 'I thought you'd planned to stay away all summer. You've been away for only a week.'

'Less than a week. I got back yesterday.' As he leaned back in his chair and regarded her narrowly, Beth felt a sense of sharp relief. So, she was not, after all, losing her reason. He had been here yesterday. That *was* him she'd seen! 'What's the matter?' he was asking her. 'Would you rather I'd stayed away?'

Beth struggled to appear indifferent. 'It doesn't much matter. I'm leaving this evening, as it happens.' The truth was that she didn't know if she was glad or sorry. Just the sight of him and his nearness had turned her limbs to jelly and reawakened that dull ache in her soul. And, though she knew she would not have traded this last chance to be with him for all the jewels of the Orient, she knew that it would now be a thousand times harder for her to climb aboard that plane tonight.

But now it was his turn to look surprised. 'You're leaving so soon? Have the papers been signed, then? I didn't expect it all to be settled so quickly.'

'Neither did I, but that lawyer of yours was really quite incredibly efficient.' She managed a small smile. 'Thank you for recommending him.'

Lorenzo shrugged off her gratitude. 'It was the least I could do.' His eyes narrowed a little. 'So Giles co-operated? I was a little worried he might refuse to sign.'

Beth nodded now, admitting to herself that that had been her own greatest fear. For her suspicion had grown that the original legal mix-up had more than likely been deliberately engineered. It was Giles, after all, who had instructed the solicitors who had drawn up the faulty document in his favour. It seemed he had deliberately cheated his own father.

Likewise, she felt sure that he had received her mother's letters, but had simply chosen to ignore them, with every intention of just leaving things as they were.

She glanced at Lorenzo. 'I'm just glad he did co-operate. Perhaps he's hoping that this one honest gesture might count in his favour when he comes up for trial.' She swallowed drily. 'But what about you?' Giles was not a subject she wished to discuss right now—and he was most definitely not what was uppermost in her mind! 'Why did you cut your holiday short? There's nothing wrong, is there?' she asked anxiously. 'Nothing's happened to Mariella?'

At her evidently sincere concern for his sister, Lorenzo shook his head and smiled across at her. 'No, nothing's happened to Mariella—at least nothing of the sort that you have in mind.' He smiled wryly. 'However, almost on our very first day in Sardinia, she managed to fall head over heels in love with the son of a very good friend of mine. Alessandro's the boy's name. He was over on holiday with his parents.'

He shrugged good-humouredly. 'So, I left them to it. Little sister definitely didn't want big brother around, and I have plenty of things to get on with here.'

For the first time in a long while Beth felt genuine pleasure. 'Good for Mariella!' she exclaimed delightedly. 'I'm really glad to hear she's got over her heartbreak and found herself a nice boy to go around with.'

For Beth had no doubt that Alessandro, if he had Lorenzo's approval, which he certainly appeared to do, must be the right sort of boy for Mariella. She had total faith in Lorenzo's judgement. Sometimes big brothers really did know best!

He was watching her closely, smiling at her pleasure. 'You see how quickly the young recover from heartbreak?' He raised one dark eyebrow, his expression growing more serious, as, in a low voice, he told her now, 'It'll be the same for you. You'll soon recover. You'll find someone new.'

It took Beth a wretched, heart-stopping moment to realise that he was referring to her recently ended engagement and not to her current distress over him.

She had to wait a moment till the tumult stilled inside her before she could answer. 'Yes, I expect I will.' Then she adjusted the hem of her caftan and added, 'But I was far from heartbroken over Alec. As I told you, I never really loved him.'

'But you were upset.' The black eyes were on her, seeming to bore like lasers right through her. 'Far more upset than you need have been.'

He paused and, as she lifted her gaze to meet his, she was totally astounded when he told her, 'I really admire you for breaking off your engagement.'

'Admire me?' Beth blinked at him. Surely she was hearing things!

'It took a great deal of courage and I greatly admire courage. It is not a quality one comes across often.'

Beth was staring at him in total bewilderment. 'But I thought you despised me for breaking my engagement.'

Lorenzo frowned. 'Despised you? No! I was sceptical at first regarding your motives, but once I knew the kind of man your fiancé had been my only feeling was admiration.' He smiled and dropped his eyes briefly to the floor, then glanced up at her once more as he told her candidly, 'I wish I'd had the courage to do likewise myself.'

Beth was now completely floored. He seemed to be speaking a different language. She leaned forward in her seat, totally baffled. 'I don't understand. What are you saying?'

'I'm saying, *cara* Beth, that if I'd had your courage, I wouldn't have ended up wasting five years of my life. I'd have ended my own ill-judged engagement before it became a total farce. Or, better still, I would never have got engaged in the first place.'

'But I thought . . . Mariella said——' Hurriedly Beth cut herself short, realising she was on the brink of a gross indiscretion.

But Lorenzo simply smiled across at her. 'So, Mariella told you all about it? I suspected she might have. She loves nothing better than discussing my love-life. But in this particular case, I'm afraid, she doesn't know what she's talking about. No one knows the truth except me.'

As Beth watched him curiously, he put to her, 'I suppose my sister told you I was heartbroken when Caterina went off with another man?' As she nodded tentatively, he shook his dark head at her. 'The truth is I was never so relieved in my life.'

As he paused for a moment Beth was suddenly certain that she was the first person ever to hear his confession. Feeling oddly privileged, yet wondering why he should choose her, she listened in silence as he continued, 'I got engaged to Caterina shortly after her sister and her parents were killed. Originally it had been her sister I'd been dating, but after the tragedy I got involved with Caterina. Not really because I wanted to. It just sort of happened. She was distraught, not surprisingly, and it was me she turned to.'

He paused to breathe deeply, his long legs stretched before him. 'I guess I was young. I didn't know any better. When she told me she couldn't live without me, I believed her. I succumbed to her pressure that we announce our engagement because I felt sorry for her and I felt it was my duty.

'But it was a big mistake. I realised that immediately. She was one of those greedy grasping females who believe that men owe them a living, and she really took me for a fool. But, as I say, I felt sorry for her... For whatever reason, I didn't have the courage to call it off. Thank heavens that, in the end, she did it for me!'

He shook his head wryly. 'That night she told me she was breaking our engagement was the one and only time I've ever got drunk. I suppose people thought I was drowning my sorrows, but what I was really doing was having the celebration of my life!'

As he came to the end of his story, he looked across at Beth. 'So, you see, not everyone has your courage. We don't all have the guts to do what you did.'

Beth frowned in disagreement. 'Your situation was different. I think what you did for that girl was admirable. Not many men would have made such a sacrifice.'

'At least I learned from my mistake.' He threw her a shrewd look. 'Having discovered to my cost just how difficult it can be to disentangle oneself from a relationship once one gets into it, I've made damned sure I steer clear of all dubious involvements. I won't get taken like that a second time.'

His expression softened. He leaned towards her. 'I hope you'll learn from your mistake, too. Keep away from selfish, manipulative men, who just want to use you for their own ends. For that's the type Alec was. You know that, don't you? The loan he made you and all his promises were just to conveniently keep you waiting there for him.'

Contempt clenched his jaw and flooded the dark eyes. 'While appearing to be the very soul of generosity, in reality he gave you nothing.' Suddenly, he touched her. 'And you deserve better than that.'

Beth gazed at him, feeling her heart weep within her. He was so good, so strong, so compassionate, so wise. Even without knowing of that final infidelity, he had summed up Alec with perfect accuracy. And she wished with all her soul that he had not come here today. The way she loved him at this moment was an agony from which she would never recover.

With his fingers, he was stroking her arm gently, sending hot and cold shivers skittering through her. And he seemed to have drawn his chair a little closer as he told her, 'Those people who criticised you for breaking off your engagement; they didn't know what the hell they were talking about. When you go back to England, tell them from me that they're nothing but a bunch of short-sighted idiots.'

Beth smiled limply. When you go back to England... Somehow, on his lips it had sounded like a death sentence. But she kept on smiling. 'I won't be seeing them. They were friends of Alec's, really, not mine.'

'I'm glad to hear it. Don't waste your time on them. Just remember, Beth, you're a girl in a million.' He smiled strangely. 'As I said, you have courage—including the courage to stand up for what you believe.'

He drew in breath, a pained look in his eyes. 'I apologise for all those things I said that night when we were back at Giles's villa after dinner. I don't blame you in the least for standing by your stepbrother. After all, you didn't know what he was up to. And you wouldn't be the girl you are if you'd betrayed him.'

Perversely, his words only deepened her pain. She dropped her eyes away, then lifted them again slowly. 'One thing that always troubled me a little... How could you ever have believed that I was involved in what was going on?'

'I never really did. I just had to test you.' He reached for her hand and squeezed it in his own. 'At the end I was simply pretending I did because I was angry with you, *cara*. Illogically angry because you'd lied to me—even though I knew you had no choice but to lie.'

He raised her hand to his lips and kissed it, sending a helpless longing shivering through her. 'Let me confess how I knew that you were completely innocent...' his eyes darkened a little '...though you may not like it.'

Beth could hardly bear to look at him. 'You don't have to...' she began. All that mattered was that he was sure she was innocent.

'I shall tell you, anyway, *cara* Beth. It is something you have a right to know.' He held her hand for a moment against his face and looked deep into her eyes as he continued. 'Ever since you arrived here, you've been under surveillance. The phone was tapped. There was always someone watching you. The work of the police, not me,' he quickly added. 'They were hoping that you might lead them to Giles.' He smiled a little sheepishly. 'As you will appreciate, it soon became clear that you knew even less than the rest of us.'

Beth shook her head, but she wasn't angry. 'I had nothing to hide, so it doesn't matter. And I suppose you could say it was all in a good cause.'

'I'm glad you see it that way.' He kissed her hand again. 'I felt a little bad about deceiving you. After all, we were both on the same side. Both of us wanted to track Giles down.' He smiled suddenly and touched her hair. 'I've rarely seen anyone quite so determined.'

'Yes, I was determined...' suddenly she faltered '...but perhaps not quite to the extent you believed.' As he frowned a little she continued, watching him, 'You seemed to think I was prepared to do anything to find Giles... All those attempts at a trade-off you kept accusing me of...'

He sat back in his seat, sighed and shook his head. 'I'm sorry about that. I misjudged you. I suppose it was because I was afraid of trusting you. I couldn't believe...' He leaned towards her again. 'Why did you let me make love to you that night?'

Beth's cheeks flushed crimson. She was lost for an answer. 'And why did you make love to me?' she countered.

He did not answer her. Instead he offered, 'Shall I tell you why I thought you did it at the time?' In the face of her silence he continued, 'I thought you'd come round to the villa that night to try to persuade me to get off Giles's back again. A mild flirtation, a few heated kisses, plus the promise of something more if I would do you this favour. But things got out of hand, they went further than you'd bargained for, and that was why you ended up angry with me.

'I know now I was wrong, that that wasn't the case, but I'm still puzzled as to why you allowed me to make love to you. You're not the type of girl to go in for casual sex.'

'No, I'm not.'

'And I'm not that type of man.' He regarded her flushed, stiff face for a moment, then took a deep breath before going on to tell her, 'You'll probably think this is very funny, but the reason I made love to you is very simple...' He paused for a tantalising moment. 'I reckon I was a little in love with you that night.'

But Beth wasn't laughing. She felt a ripple of goose-pimples. 'I was a little in love with you, too,' she confessed.

There was a seemingly endless silence, the only sound her breathing, then she sensed rather than saw him move towards her. She shivered as his fingers slid through her hair. 'And now?' he was asking. 'Are you still a little in love?'

Suddenly Beth could not bear to look at him. She closed her eyes. Her heart was pounding. 'No,' she answered. 'No, I'm not. If you want to know the truth——'

'I love you very much.' His hand tightened around hers as he seemed to finish the sentence for her. But, miraculously, Beth realised, he was speaking for himself. 'That's why I came back— to tell you that I love you.'

Beth opened her eyes, which were brimming with tears now, as he reached for her and drew her to her feet. Then with a sigh he was flinging his arms around her, as though to bind her to him for that eternity she could no longer bear to imagine without him.

And again and again he whispered in her hair. 'I love you, Beth. I love you, Beth.'

It was a long time later that Beth suddenly remembered that she hadn't received a call from the airport.

'It's just as well, for you're not going anywhere,' Lorenzo insisted when she told him. 'The next time you climb on to an aeroplane, I'm going to be climbing on it right behind you.'

Beth smiled at the seriousness with which he'd said it, but behind the smile her heart stood still. Did he mean it? Or was he joking? He had told her that he loved her, but once, a long time ago, he had also told her that he believed love to be a transitory thing.

'Alas, it happens...love dies all too frequently...it is something we have to learn to live with.' Remembering these words, Beth shivered with fear. Once she could have suffered almost anything, but she could not bear to lose him now.

They were lying on the bed, amid a tangle of bedclothes, two naked bodies sated with love. He had carried her to the bedroom and laid her there gently, kissing her, caressing her, whispering his love. Then he had lain beside her and pressed her against him, so that she could feel the hunger of his loins. And then they had made love, endlessly, passionately. And then they had made love all over again.

With his lips now he kissed her, his hands caressing her breasts, and at his touch she felt raw excitement burst within her. Every nerve-end in her body seemed to shimmer.

His dark head bent over her, his eyes black and smiling. 'Did you hear what I said to you, *mia cara*? Wherever you're planning to go, I'm planning to go with you.'

Beth touched his face, her heart alight with love for him. 'And what do you plan to do in London?' she asked. 'That's the only place I'm planning on going.'

'What do I plan to do?' He seemed to think about it for a moment, as his hand swept down to caress her thighs. Then he told her calmly, 'Why, I think I'll just have a leisurely look around—meet some of the people and see some of the places that my wife used to know before she met me. And, of course, help her to wind up her business interests there.'

As she blinked back at him, dumbfounded, he added mischievously, 'That is, of course, if she agrees to be my wife.' Then his eyes grew serious. He leaned across her and pushed the hair back from her face. 'This is a proposal, *cara mia*. Kindly put me out of my misery and say yes.'

She could not speak. She merely nodded. She felt as though her heart would burst from her chest.

He kissed her eyes. 'I love you,' he told her.

Beth held her breath. 'I love you, too.'

'So, you've found your voice!' He hugged her to him. 'I love you more than you'll ever know.' Then his eyes grew serious. 'And this love is special. It's the kind of love that lasts for eternity. So, I'm warning you, if you want out of this relationship, speak now or forever hold your peace.'

Beth pressed against him. 'Never! Never! I love you more than I love my life.'

Then she gasped as he kissed her, drowning in her love for him, and suddenly there was no more need for words between them.

And Beth knew in her heart that from now until forever this man who made her heart sing with happiness within her would be the most wonderful man in the whole world to love.

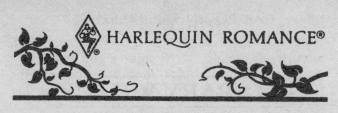

HARLEQUIN ROMANCE®

**Harlequin Romance
knows love can be dangerous!**

Don't miss
TO LOVE AND PROTECT (#3223)
by Kate Denton,
the October title in

THE BRIDAL COLLECTION

THE GROOM'S life was in peril.
THE BRIDE was hired to help him.
BUT THEIR WEDDING was *more* than
a business arrangement!

Available this month in
The Bridal Collection
JACK OF HEARTS (#3218)
by Heather Allison
Wherever Harlequin books are sold.

WED-6

HARLEQUIN PRESENTS®

BARBARY WHARF

**An exciting six-book series, one title per month
beginning in October, by bestselling author**

Set in the glamorous and fast-paced world of international
journalism, BARBARY WHARF will take you from the
Sentinel's hectic newsroom to the most thrilling cities in the
world. You'll meet media tycoon Nick Caspian and his
adversary Gina Tyrrell, whose dramatic story of passion and
heartache develops throughout the six-book series.

In book one, BESIEGED (#1498), you'll also meet Hazel and
Piet. Hazel's always had a good word to say about everyone.
Well, almost. She just can't stand Piet Van Leyden, Nick's
chief architect and one of the most arrogant know-it-alls she's
ever met! As far as Hazel's concerned, Piet's a twentieth-
century warrior, and she's the one being besieged!

Don't miss the sparks in the first BARBARY WHARF
book, BESIEGED (#1498), available in October from
Harlequin Presents.

BARB-S

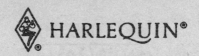 **HARLEQUIN®**

THE TAGGARTS OF TEXAS!

Harlequin's Ruth Jean Dale brings you
THE TAGGARTS OF TEXAS!

Those Taggart men—strong, sexy and hard to resist...

You've met Jesse James Taggart in FIREWORKS!
Harlequin Romance #3205 (July 1992)

Now meet Trey Smith—he's THE RED-BLOODED YANKEE!
Harlequin Temptation #413 (October 1992)

Then there's Daniel Boone Taggart in SHOWDOWN!
Harlequin Romance #3242 (January 1993)

And finally the Taggarts who started it all—in LEGEND!
Harlequin Historical #168 (April 1993)

Read all the Taggart romances!
Meet all the Taggart men!

Available wherever Harlequin books are sold.

If you missed *Fireworks!* (July 1992) and would like to order it, please send your name, address, zip or postal code, along with a check or money order for $2.89 (please do not send cash), plus 75¢ postage and handling ($1.00 in Canada) for each book ordered, payable to Harlequin Reader Service to:

In the U.S.	In Canada
3010 Walden Avenue	P.O. Box 609
P.O. Box 1325	Fort Erie, Ontario
Buffalo, NY 14269-1325	L2A 5X3

Please specify book title with your order.
Canadian residents add applicable federal and provincial taxes.

WELCOME TO

The quintessential small town, where everyone
knows everybody else!

Finally, books that capture the pleasure
of tuning in to your favorite TV show!

Join your friends at Tyler in the eighth book, BACHELOR'S PUZZLE by Ginger
Chambers, available in October.

*What do Tyler's librarian and a cosmopolitan architect have in common? What
does the coroner's office have to reveal?*

GREAT READING...GREAT SAVINGS...
AND A FABULOUS FREE GIFT!

Each book set in Tyler is a self-contained love story; together, the twelve novels
stitch the fabric of the community. You can't miss the Tyler books on the shelves
because the covers honor the old American tradition of quilting; each cover
depicts a patch of the large Tyler quilt!

And you can receive a FABULOUS GIFT, ABSOLUTELY FREE, by collecting
proofs-of-purchase found in each Tyler book, *and* use our Tyler coupons to save
on your next TYLER book purchase.

If you missed *Whirlwind* (March), *Bright Hopes* (April), *Wisconsin Wedding* (May), *Monkey
Wrench* (June), *Blazing Star* (July), *Sunshine* (August) or *Arrowpoint* (September) and would
like to order them, send your name, address, zip or postal code, along with a check or money
order for $3.99 (please do not send cash), plus 75¢ postage and handling ($1.00 in Canada)
for each book ordered, payable to Harlequin Reader Service, to:

In the U.S.

3010 Walden Avenue
P.O. Box 1325
Buffalo, NY 14269-1325

In Canada

P.O. Box 609
Fort Erie, Ontario
L2A 5X3

Please specify book title(s) with your order.
Canadian residents add applicable federal and provincial taxes.

TYLER-8